DEAD WHALES TELL NO TALES

To Natalie—

Best wishes,

Ron Lovell

8/18/00

A Thomas Martindale Mystery

DEAD WHALES TELL NO TALES

Ron Lovell

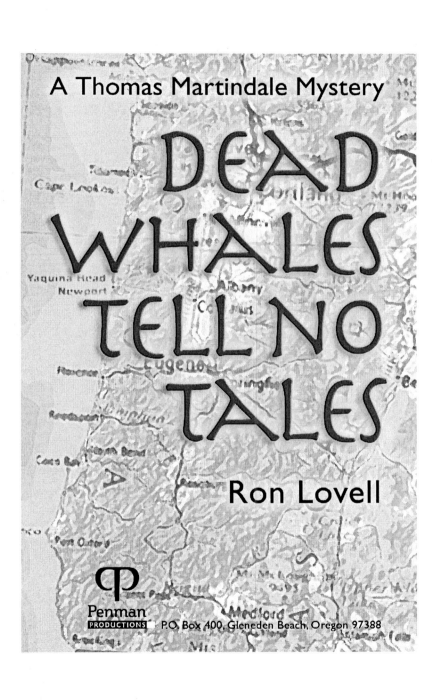

Penman
PRODUCTIONS P.O. Box 400, Gleneden Beach, Oregon 97388

Special thanks to John Byrne and Bruce Mate

~ ~ ~

SECOND EDITION

Penman Productions, Gleneden Beach, Oregon
Copyright © 2006 by Ronald P. Lovell
First edition published by Sunstone Press, 2003.

Published in the United States
by Penman Productions, Gleneden Beach, Oregon.

The events, people, and incidents in this story are the sole product
of the author's imagination. The story is fictional and any resemblance
to individuals living or dead is purely coincidental.

Printed in the United States of America
Library of Congress Control Number: 2006904309
ISBN: 0-9767978-3-6

Cover and book designer: Liz Kingslien
Editor: Mardelle Kunz
Cover photo: istock.com
Author photo: Dennis Wolverton

1

THURSDAY, APRIL 16

I HEARD THE NOISE before I actually saw who was making it. On most days, only traffic sounds from the nearby Yaquina Bay Bridge and the cries of seabirds circling the bay pierce the quiet of the parking lot at the university's Marine Center.

Today, however, that calm was broken by yelling and whistling and sawing and the snap of a staple gun coming from the far end of the lot. I parked my car and got out, my curiosity causing me to stop and look to where a dozen or so men and women were attaching placards to wooden poles.

"What the hell?" I muttered.

Demonstrations, highly unusual in Oregon, are very rare in the small town of Newport. In a few minutes, I could make out some of the words on the signs and the whole thing became clear: "Save the Whales," "Nuke" something I couldn't determine, and "Send Eskimos" to someplace that wasn't legible.

These people were preparing their messages for delegates to a conference sponsored by the International Whaling Commission that would begin tomorrow at the center. IWC meetings always attract conservationists who are rabid in their opposition to whaling and the countries that still practice it. But I was surprised to see them in this remote part of the

Oregon coast. The normally prevailing isolation that university officials had counted on to aid in dispassionate deliberations on whale population totals and hunting quotas had definitely been penetrated.

I turned from the would-be protesters and stepped into the roadway without looking toward the entry gate. If I hadn't been distracted by the commotion, I might have seen the dark green Mercedes in time to avoid being nearly run over by it; almost too late I saw the familiar boxy grill and distinctive hood emblem of the car only a few feet away. The driver barely slowed as the large sedan touched my briefcase and actually turned me around.

I didn't see the driver's face and could only make out the blurred image of a vanity license plate: DKTR K. The driver screeched to a halt at the other end of the lot, but did not get out of the car. I curbed my urge to run down and confront him—or her—because I was late and needed to get to class. After all, only my pride was hurt.

I walked up the path to the front door and through the aquarium area of the center. As usual, it was crowded with visitors looking at the fish tanks and other displays. Kids were playing with the octopus and starfish in the pool near the entrance doors. I walked past the cases of illegal ivory and confiscated cans of whale meat. Except for the Japanese lettering on the labels and their exotic contents, the cans might be tuna sold at any grocery. How ironic that the fate of the whales whose meat had been processed to go into these cans would be decided tomorrow, only a few feet away in the auditorium.

I reached the door of the classroom with a few minutes to spare and squared my shoulders before going in. I'm always just a little nervous the first day of class. Even though I've been teaching for a long time, I always feel the tiniest bit of stage fright when I face a roomful of strangers. I feel the need to connect with students on the first day, but they seldom respond. They never laugh at my attempts at humor or react much when I greet them individually, as I hand out the course syllabus. Their collective dourness makes me feel like a nightclub comedian trying to liven up a bunch of unsmiling accountants and their wives in the smoke-filled cocktail lounge of a Holiday Inn in North Dakota—in spite of the genius of the jokes and the help of a drummer who uses his cymbal after every punch line (vada vi! vada voom!), they just sit there while I die on stage.

But today would be different, I firmly believed. The class was composed of graduate students, only a few undergraduates, and a smattering of Newport residents. Maybe I'd have more of a chance.

In the first place, I wouldn't be teaching alone. I was part of a four-professor team conducting a three-day seminar on "Whales and Other Creatures of the Deep" being held in conjunction with the IWC conference on whaling. I was supposed to be on sabbatical leave to do some writing, but came because my old friend Susan Foster, a marine biologist, asked me to present several sessions on nature writing. She and two others will be on the team with me.

I opened the door, walked in, greeted my colleagues, and went to work. With Randy Webb, a journalism colleague who teaches photography, I started distributing outlines while Susan presided from the front of the conference room. Twenty-five people had signed up, but only eighteen were sitting around the large oblong table.

"Good morning. Hello." I made my way around the table greeting one student and then another; most smiled in response, but said nothing. I was on one side of the room, Randy on the other.

"How ya doin'?" I paused in front of a remarkable looking young woman whose dark hair and beautiful features would attract attention anywhere.

"Trog won't need an outline. He's here to assist me," she said. "I'm Mara."

"Pardon me?"

"Trog, my . . . er . . . friend here. He isn't taking the class for credit."

For the first time I noticed the burly man seated next to her. He was big: muscular tending toward heavyset, with small eyes that were set wrong in his pockmarked face, one slightly higher than the other.

"Okay, but he can have one. Paper's pretty cheap, and it will give him something to read." I offered a syllabus to him, but he shook his head and refused to accept it. "Suit yourself."

I moved on, a bit unnerved by the odd combination of pretty girl and ugly guy. Theirs almost seemed like a body-guard arrangement, but I dismissed that as too odd in a class setting.

"Hello. How are you today?" I stopped in front of an older woman dressed in a flowered smock and wearing a large sun hat.

"Edna Ruth Meyers." She held out her hand, which I shook. "I hope you'll be willing to read my book manuscript while I'm in your class."

I imagined she was an older-than-average student taking the course for something to do. I knew from past experience with the Edna Ruth's of this world that her manuscript—and I want to be kind in saying this—probably wasn't marketable. She was probably trying to get it published because some-one—a friend, a relative—had once told her she really had tal-ent. "If you get this published," they no doubt had said, "I'll be sure to buy a copy."

Past experience cast doubt on that happening, but part of my job as a teacher is to encourage and help my students, so I was vague in my answer. "Oh, I think that's great that you've done a book-length work," I said. "That takes dedication and discipline. But we should concentrate on the work for this class first. We aren't going to have much time."

Her face fell and she frowned; I hadn't made a hit with that dose of realism, so I walked on to the next student.

"Professor Martindale, I've been looking forward to meeting you. I've read your textbooks and heard a lot about you. Scott Szabo. I was hoping you would take me under your wing and help me with my writing."

A tall, good-looking young man with curly blond hair and a close cropped beard to match shook my hand—the graduate student as fawning supplicant. Szabo seemed at first glance to be trying to ingratiate himself to me in hopes that it would lead to a good grade. Most graduate students are obsessed with grades. In their minds, anything less than an "A" is flunking. I had learned long ago to wait until I saw the quality of a student's work before becoming a mentor.

"Good to meet you," I said noncommittally.

Randy and I reached the other end of the table at the same time and moved back to stand against the rear wall of the room. Just then, John Strong walked into the room and stepped up to the lectern. Susan was now standing slightly to his left, talking in an animated way to an older man who was somewhat agitated. The man was glaring at her and punctuating his words by pointing a finger at her face. When Strong started to speak, they both stopped talking.

"Good morning. Welcome to MB 509, 'Whales and Other Creatures of the Deep.' We're pleased to have you enrolled in this special three-day seminar here at the university Marine

Center. My name is John Strong, director of the center, and your professor of record. Assisting me will be Susan Foster, associate professor of marine biology . . ."

Susan stepped forward and smiled.

". . . Howard Phelps, professor of marine biology, and a world-renowned authority on marine mammals . . ."

The older man stepped forward, his finger no longer pointing at Susan. He did not wave or smile, however.

". . . Tom Martindale, associate professor of journalism at the university and a former magazine investigative reporter . . ."

I raised one arm to call attention to myself.

". . . and Randy Webb, assistant professor of journalism."

Randy stepped forward and raised both arms. Assistant professors have to be more demonstrative to get noticed.

"We're here to tell you about whales and other creatures of the ocean, like otters and seals and sharks," Strong began. "Our two marine biologists will cover that. Professor Martindale will discuss how to write about these wonderful creatures, and Professor Webb will explain how to photograph them. Then, tomorrow, you will get the chance to see some of the creatures up close, then write and take photos of them the day after that.

"Also tomorrow, you'll have the opportunity to attend sessions of a conference on whale research and population that is taking place here at the center under the auspices of the International Whaling Commission. I'm chairman of that meeting, so I'll need to be in and out of here today to see to arrangements, but you'll be in very good hands while I'm away. You have your course outlines in front of you. Read them and we'll answer any questions you have at the break. We'll get started with Professor Foster, who will give you a general introduction to whales. Sue."

Susan looked good in her designer jeans and blue work shirt over white turtleneck ensemble. She wore little makeup and had pulled her hair back into a bun. Seeing her reminded me how much I cared for her, in spite of everything that had happened. We had dated several years ago when she first came to campus, but things hadn't gone very well.

She drank a little too much and once, when we were arguing over that, she blurted out that she thought I was too old for her, and, far worse, she said I wasn't a good lover. She had been drinking at the time and used that as an excuse when she apologized later. Although I sloughed off her remarks, they did hurt me—a lot. No man likes to have his masculinity questioned.

We dropped the subject, but, needless to say, gradually drifted apart. Even though she apologized for the sex remark, I decided I didn't like what the drinking did to her. Then she moved to Newport, and we rarely saw one another. When we did, however, we gradually resumed the easy banter of two people who like each other. The things she had said were still there in some little compartment of my mind, but I didn't want to let them destroy our friendship.

As she stepped up to the lectern, Sue pulled her glasses down from their perch on her head and began to read from her notes, looking up from time to time to make eye contact with the students.

"Man's affinity to whales may be explained in part by the similarities in their basic physiological characteristics," she began. "Both are warm-blooded, air-breathing mammals. The linkage ends here, however, because of the whale's habitat. It is born and weaned, and it breeds and dies at sea.

"The whale is in constant motion in water of great depth, but it must come to the surface periodically to breathe or blow. The body of a whale—smooth, nearly without hair, torpedo-shaped—encounters little resistance in accomplishing its primary purpose: to swim. A whale propels its rigid body forward by powerful strokes of its tail, which is expanded at the end into two horizontal flukes. Whales alter the direction of their thrust by swinging their tails sideways. Between their skeletal structure and skin, whales have a layer of blubber that acts as insulation and helps to retain body heat."

As she started her lecture, Randy projected photos of whales on the screen to Susan's left. The beautiful pictures and the details she presented captured the attention of the students immediately. Most were taking notes, a few placed tape recorders on the table in front of them.

"All of these characteristics have added to their fascination. They are the only great creatures that man has not had to fear. Aside from the fictional Moby Dick, few whales have been known to attack men. Conversely, man has turned out to pose the greatest danger to whales."

Susan went on to talk about how whales have been caught and killed for their oil, meat, and baleen, the long protuberances in the mouths of some species which help them strain their food before eating it. She noted that whales were hunted today primarily for their meat because spring steel had long ago replaced baleen in most products. The killing of whales for their meat was especially true with Japan. She said that Japan's near fanatical desire to continue its commercial whaling resulted from the actions of an American.

In 1945, faced with feeding a starving nation, General Douglas MacArthur, supreme commander of the Allied Occupation Forces in Japan, ordered the Japanese to repair their old oil tankers and convert them to whaling ships. The American government financed the venture and was repaid in whale oil. The Japanese people were given the whale meat to eat and many acquired a taste for it.

"With continued support from the Japanese government since the 1950s, the whaling industry has grown and prospered," she continued. "It has also acquired the domestic political clout to survive. Even the steady rise of international opposition to whaling has not diminished the willingness of successive Japanese governments to support the whalers and their close ally, the fishing industry."

She said the Japanese government had conducted a carefully planned campaign against some members of the International Whaling Commission to swing the vote in order to be able to continue whaling. The IWC was established in 1946 to regulate whaling and attempt to protect the stocks of whales in danger of extinction. Gradually over the years, more and more species of whales have come under IWC protection and are no longer killed. In 1986, the IWC enacted a worldwide moratorium on commercial whaling, although allowing some subsistence whaling by a few indigenous groups.

This has made Japan a bit more desperate to get whale meat, hence its arrangement with countries like Iceland to buy the meat after that nation has completed its "scientific research" on whales the it has killed.

"They eat red whale meat in much the same way Westerners eat beef, for example. They resent efforts by the U.S. and other nations in the IWC to stop them from obtaining whale meat. Although Americans and others deify whales as great creatures with almost mystical characteristics, the Japanese simply think of them as larger versions of cows or chickens. They see whales as nothing more than a food resource, and they have no hesitancy in killing a whale, as a Westerner would not think twice about slaughtering a cow or wringing the neck of a chicken."

Susan stopped lecturing and pushed her glasses back up onto her head. The students put down their pens, a few stopped their tape recorders, as well. It had been a good beginning.

"We'll pause here for questions."

A hand went up from a skinny kid on the other side of the table. "Will any of this be on the test?"

There was an audible moan from the graduate students in the room. This was a typical question from many undergraduates—one that disproves the maxim that there are no stupid questions.

"No," she consulted a seating chart, "Peter, is it?"

"Yeah, Peter Turley."

"We aren't having tests *per se*, as your course syllabus says. You'll be graded on your written work later." She looked around the room for more questions.

Scott Szabo raised his hand, glancing at me as he spoke. "This meeting tomorrow here at the center. How does it relate to what you said about whale hunting?"

"Good question, Scott. It is very closely related. The figures on whale population for some species presented here may be used by the IWC later to set quotas on how many whales can be hunted. That's why I urge all of you to attend as much of the conference as you can. We'll set aside some seats for you at the rear of the auditorium. Any more questions?"

Everyone else remained silent.

"Seeing no more hands, I'd like to turn things over to Professor Howard Phelps, a distinguished professor of marine biology at the center and at the university. He will talk to you about other creatures of the deep."

Phelps moved briskly to the lectern, placing a thick folder on its tilted surface. Although he was nice looking, the ravages of age were encroaching on Phelps's fine, almost delicate features.

He seemed to be trying to fight back, by wearing his thick, gray hair rather longish and choosing modish wire-rimmed glasses. The hair, the glasses, the bow tie, and the tweed jacket with leather patches on the elbows made him look like Central Casting's idea of the perfect "Mr. Chips." This idealized impression vanished as soon as he opened his mouth.

"There is much to disagree with in Professor Foster's statement. But I'll get to that in a moment. First, I do not wish to have any of my remarks taped." He glowered at the students with the tape recorders, and they quickly pushed the OFF buttons.

"I'll brook no talking in class or gum chewing." He glared at Peter Turley, who just about unhinged his jaw in his haste to remove the offending wad of gum that was residing there. "I find it helpful to have my students sit up straight when they are in my class."

The assembled group seemed to square its shoulders as one, except Trog, who looked sullenly at Phelps and remained hunched over.

Phelps was definitely not Mr. Chips, but more like an academic Mr. Hyde.

"Very well. With those tiresome details out of the way, let me say something else. I must take exception to the remarks of my esteemed colleague Professor Foster. She has given you a misleading, if not erroneous, picture of the Japanese and whaling. That great nation needs whale meat for its people to survive. To say otherwise is not only wrong, it is slanderous!"

2

HOWARD PHELPS HAD COMMITTED the most unpardonable sin of all in the academic world: he had criticized and contradicted a colleague in front of students—not just one student, but a whole class of them.

I glanced at Sue, who looked stricken. She seemed about to speak, but apparently thought better of it and just gazed at Phelps, trying not to display any emotion. Every once in a while, she wrote something on a pad, as if preparing a rebuttal.

The students shifted uneasily in their seats; some put down their pens and crossed their arms—seeming to make a point of defying Phelps by not writing down what he was saying. If he sensed their disrespect, Phelps did not show it. He went on with his regular lecture on marine mammals as if nothing had happened. He finished and just as it was time for questions, a distinguished-looking man in a stylish, double-breasted suit appeared in the doorway. Once Phelps saw him, he held up both hands as if to fend off the class and headed toward the door. Phelps took hold of his arm and steered him out into the hall.

Susan stood hesitantly, perplexed all over again by her colleague's action. "It's time for our morning break. We'll reconvene at ten forty-five to hear Professor Martindale talk about writing."

The students got up and filed slowly toward the door. Randy Webb sidled over to me. "What was that all about?"

"I'm not sure. I'll see what I can find out."

I waited until the students were out of earshot before walking up to Susan. "What's with your friend Phelps? He's acting a bit odd, don't you think?"

"Boy, you can say that again. I'm a bit surprised myself. Howard is an old professor of mine. I used to idolize him, but lately he's gotten kind of, I don't know, overly argumentative. He's ready to criticize everything I do."

"Occupational hazard, I should think. When the student outshines the professor, it's sometimes hard for the professor to take. I see it all the time in my department. But what he did here this morning is inexcusable. I mean, you don't act like that in front of students."

"Howard's really mad at me. He thinks I've been too hard on the Japanese. He thinks I've taken a shortcut in compiling my data about Bowhead whales and Minke whales. He thinks the results will be harmful to the Japanese whaling people. You know they're going to be here at the meeting. I don't know, I guess he wants to impress them or something."

"I thought scientists were supposed to be on the side of the whales."

"Don't I wish. I hate to say it, but some of them seem to come up with results that support the side that pays them. But Howard has never done that. He's an old pro—plenty of kudos and publications. He doesn't need to impress anybody."

"Can he hurt you on this, Sue?"

She hesitated and shook her head. "No, I don't think so. He's chairing my promotion committee, but I don't think he'd let something like this affect that."

Susan was interrupted by a loud knock on the door frame. Even though the door was open, we couldn't see who was there. Another knock. I was standing closest to the doorway, so

I walked around and found myself looking at the large, mus-
cled neck of a man who, when I followed that neck up to his
head, must have been six foot six or taller. He had tree stump
arms and legs and a bullet-shaped head. And he was decidedly
Japanese. I caught my breath and stepped aside.

Susan's eyes widened briefly before she overcame her surprise. "Were you looking for me?"

"Professor Susan Foster, I am Mr. Jima. I represent His
Excellency, Minister Nagamo, who requests the honor of your
presence in the director's conference room at this time."

"Japanese Fisheries Minister Nagamo?"

The large mountain nodded slightly.

"Tom, do you mind? I really should pay a courtesy call on him
and the other delegates. Can you start things off after the break? I'll
come back at noon to send the students to lunch and go over that
material I promised you for your writing exercises tomorrow."

"Of course. I'll handle everything here."

The two departed, and I decided to use the twenty minutes
or so before class resumed to go outside into the fresh air. It
was a lovely spring day, and I could smell the ocean even
before I rounded the corner of the building to see it. The sun's
rays were making the water of Yaquina Bay sparkle as I looked
across it to the town of Newport. The parking lot next to the
center was filling up with the cars of both tourists and atten-
dees arriving early for the conference. The demonstrators were
nowhere to be seen. The green Mercedes was still parked at the
far end of the lot. Was it too late to confront the driver? I
decided I had better things to do with my time.

I walked through the public area of the center, then opened
the "Staff Only" door and traversed the long hall past faculty
offices on my way back to the seminar room. Loud shouting
was coming from the door marked "Howard Phelps, Ph.D."

"You killed him, Phelps, just as if you drove a knife through his heart."

"My dear sir, I don't know what you are talking about."

I'm as interested in gossip and scandal as any red-blooded reporter, so I slowed my gait to a virtual crawl in order to hear more.

"You ruined his life, Phelps, with all your . . ."

Just as the professor's visitor was getting to the good part, someone slammed the heavy door shut, instantly muffling the sound. I hurried on, somewhat distressed over what I had heard.

~ ~ ~

The class had reassembled by the time I got to the room, most with their pens and pads at the ready.

"Welcome back to the second half of this morning's program. By the way, I don't mind if you tape my remarks." Might as well distance myself from Phelps right away. I paused for effect, then began my formal lecture.

"Writing about the sea and the creatures that live in it is one of the most satisfying, tantalizing, and difficult tasks for any writer. Experts agree that we only know about ten to twenty percent of the secrets of the sea, in spite of the fact that oceans cover three quarters of the surface of the earth. And within this murky realm, no creature is more awe inspiring than the whale. That's where the satisfying and tantalizing part of your job as writers comes in.

"If you're like me, you love whales. Since I read *Moby Dick* in high school, whales have always symbolized nature at its best. Gigantic in size, yet gentle in disposition, whales play their role in the natural world in an almost unassuming way—if anything can be unassuming when it is fifty feet long and weighs forty tons!"

As I spoke, Randy began to project more whale photographs on the screen. These striking images added pizzazz to my lecture, and I appreciated his willingness to show them.

"The difficulty for a nature writer—as for a scientist—comes from working in an often harsh environment and in actually seeing the huge creatures you are expected to write about. These big guys do, after all, spend much of their time under water."

More photos appeared on-screen and the students seemed enthralled.

"In journalism, you are taught to be objective. In nature writing, you need to be objective—but only to a point. You can be like the editorial writer who observes the battle from the hill." I paused for effect. "Then, after it is over, goes down and kills the wounded."

They laughed. God bless graduate students.

"What I mean is that you are liable to become so enthralled in your work that the mystery and beauty of the world around you will, at times, overcome your objectivity. But that's all right. You can't be a good nature writer if you don't, from time to time, express your love of the out-of-doors and all the creatures living on the land, in the sea, and in the air."

I turned next to the nuts and bolts of this kind of writing, then outlined our plans for field research around Yaquina Bay tomorrow and the beginning of their writing the day after that. I finished precisely at noon. Since Sue hadn't returned, I dismissed the class and asked them to come back at one thirty for Randy Webb's session on nature photography.

After I couldn't locate Susan at her office or lab, I decided to drive home for lunch.

3

THE HOUSE I WAS RENTING was about two miles north of the city. It overlooked a cove that had once been a cave before its roof had fallen in. The high sides of the cove made it isolated and spectacular. Even though all of Oregon's beaches are public, few people find their way to this remote section. It was all but invisible from the road, and visitors would have to cross private property—my yard and those near me—to get there.

I drove up the narrow gravel road and noticed, for the first time, the mailbox in front of the house two doors away. "H. Phelps," it read.

"I'll be damned," I muttered to myself. So Susan's disagreeable old mentor was practically a neighbor. I pulled into my turnaround and got out.

"Shit." It was beginning to rain. So much for the morning's promise of a nice day. But that was Oregon in the spring. I had thought earlier about walking down to the beach after I'd eaten my lunch, but that wasn't going to happen now. I got my mail out of the box and entered the house.

As I waited for my soup to heat, I looked around the small house. You could see at least part of every room from where I was standing in the corner of the kitchen: two small bedrooms, a bathroom, and a living room separated from the kitchen by one of those old-fashioned breakfast bars with stools arranged on one side.

I have always considered surroundings to be very important—both as a person and as a writer. I have always required a good writing area—in this case it was an old wooden harvest table with plenty of surface space. I had placed it next to the floor-to-ceiling windows on the west, and in the corner so that my back would be to the tall bookshelves on the south wall. I like the feeling of security you get from sitting in a corner. Besides, I could catch a glimpse of the ocean off the edge of the yard. Far from distracting, the view was reassuring and comforting.

I liked having a lot of books around, as well. In this case, most of them belonged to my historian landlord. Their contents didn't interest me all that much, but I took pleasure in seeing them. I had brought some of my own from Corvallis—enough to fill the back seat.

I had added a few other things to motivate me in my writing: a series of whale posters I had found last year at a used books store in San Francisco. They weren't framed yet, but their cardboard mountings made them stiff enough to stand, mostly on bookshelves and assorted tables. It was inspirational to have the subject of my works-in-progress where I could keep an eye on them.

I tested the soup and poured it into a bowl, then sat at the bar and ate it and an apple. I then walked out onto the small deck, intending to look into the cove. The rocky sides were so steep that I couldn't get down from this point to investigate, and I couldn't see the beach or the edge of the water from my house, but I did notice that birds were circling and cawing noisily.

"That's funny. Must be a storm coming. Wind and high surf. Pretty late in the year for either."

The rain's intensity increased and drove me back inside. The phone was ringing in the small kitchen.

"Tom. I'm glad I caught you. It's Susan."

"Hi, Susan. I came home for some lunch."

"I'm sorry I didn't make it back in time—it was Phelps again. He burst in on my meeting with the minister, then demanded we both go see the director. Things escalated and I said some pretty harsh things."

"How bad did it get?"

"I guess I pretty much blew my stack. So much that I think I should try to mend some fences this afternoon. You know, many of these people will be on my promotion and tenure committee."

"Yeah. They can screw you if they want to—and with very little provocation."

"This is all I need. Today of all days. I wanted to spend some time on my presentation for tomorrow."

"Don't worry about that now. Is there any way I could photocopy the material you were going to give me for those writing exercises I'm putting together for tomorrow?"

"I've already done that. I'll leave the material I was going to go over with you with my secretary Mildred. She's in an office two doors from me. I'll highlight key stuff in yellow. Okay?"

"Sure, Sue. The last thing I want to do is to hassle you on a day like today. I'll pick up the stuff and get back to you if I need anything else."

What a jerk this Phelps guy is, I thought, after I hung up the phone.

I've found the academic system to be full of people like him, people who make it their sworn duty in life to make trouble for those they fear or are jealous of. I'd gotten my own promotion from assistant to associate professor several years before without as much trouble as I'd feared. But things are set up so that you can be done in by the proverbial thousand cuts and never know who's wielding the knives.

I put the dishes and pan in the sink, then on second thought, I decided to wash them. It wouldn't take long, and I'd be happy later if I didn't have to come home to a sink full of dirty dishes.

I locked up and ran through the heavy rain to my car. As I completed the turnaround back to the road, I again noticed the circling birds in the sky, close to the water's edge. I promised myself a look tonight or tomorrow or whenever the rain let up—something had attracted their attention.

After making sure that Randy got his session going, I spent the afternoon in the library, going over Susan's material and planning my presentations for the rest of the seminar. The center wasn't very busy; the students were probably studying elsewhere and staff members were evidently preparing for the conference. I couldn't get my mind off Susan and her problems. I hated to see bad things happen to my friends, especially under circumstances that were unfair and unprofessional. I decided to talk to Phelps myself to see if I could get a feel for what he was up to and whether he was out to get Sue.

As I drove slowly to my house, I had to swerve to avoid a small sports car heading in the opposite direction at high speed. Because the tall trees shading the east side of the road made it darker, I couldn't get a clear view of the driver. I only caught a glimpse of dark glasses and a curly blond beard.

It was about four fifteen when I pulled into the turnaround of my house. It had stopped raining but was still fairly drippy, with large drops falling from the fir trees that lined the road, and wide, fairly deep puddles of water I tried to avoid as I walked along. I walked up to Phelps's lane and noticed immediately that all the lights were on in his house. A car was in the carport. The newspaper was still in the tube at the driveway. I didn't look in his mailbox.

His gray house was a shingled, saltbox style—very neat and comfortable looking. Each window was fronted by a box planted with red geraniums. The sidewalk up to his door was covered with leaves, pine needles, and a few wet, wind-damaged blossoms. I knocked at the door, first using the heavy brass whale ornament bolted there, then resorting to my own knuckles in exasperation when no one opened the door.

"Professor Phelps. Anybody home? Hello. Hello."

Nothing.

I decided to risk his wrath and walked around to the rear to try another door. A large cedar deck was attached to the back of the house, positioned to take advantage of a view of the cove and the ocean beyond. I ignored the spectacular scenery for the moment, concentrating on the route to his back door. As I walked along the gravel path, it started to sprinkle again. True Oregonian that I am, I ignored it.

The deck was, as expected, neat, with a precise arrangement of tables, chairs, and more planters. A barbecue covered with a canvas tarp stood in one corner.

This door had glass in it, so I could peer in as I knocked. "Dr. Phelps. It's Thomas Martindale. I'm teaching the class with you at the center. Dr. Phelps!"

Again, nothing.

I pressed my face up to the window and shielded my eyes from the glare of the ocean. Typical of the Oregon coast, the sun had suddenly broken through the clouds and was shining directly onto the glass. Through the woven wood blinds, I could make out a dining area and the kitchen beyond that. The table was clear except for a cup that seemed to have coffee spilled down its sides and on the surface below it. The kitchen sideboards were gleaming and empty of everything but a coffee maker.

I continued to knock while I tried the doorknob. Phelps struck me as someone who would just as soon have you arrested for breaking and entering as look at you, but I really wanted to talk to him. The knob wouldn't budge.

As I turned to walk back across the deck, something caught my eye, something white. I walked toward it, noticing for the first time that the steep drop-off into the cove started just beyond the grass. When I bent over to pick up what turned out to be a sheet of rain-soaked paper, I saw something large and gray on the sand far below. It was impossible to see into the old roofless cave until you got this close to the edge.

I smoothed out the paper. It seemed to be the cover sheet of a report, its upper left corner torn jaggedly where it had been stapled. "Current Whale Population Census" was the title. "#2 of 2" was typed at the bottom with the university logo in the center and a dark brown splotch on the right near the top.

The noise of the birds, suddenly louder, drew me closer to the edge overlooking the cove. At the bottom, I could still only make out a large gray mass of something. What was it? God, could it be a beached whale? Gray whales were migrating north this time of year. Susan had included a clipping about the start of their annual migration in the material she had given me.

I stuffed the paper in my pocket and started toward the cove; the possibility that I was about to see a whale up close caused all thoughts of Phelps to evaporate like beach fog on a sunny day. A narrow path ran from the rim of the cove to the bottom. I had to walk slowly and carefully along the muddy and sandy path, which seemed to crumble with each step I took. I kept falling against the side, no doubt staining my chinos. I was glad I had left my blue blazer in the car. I even got a spot of sand on the whale tie I had been wearing all day. The wet sand wasn't doing much for my black loafers either. At one point, I nearly fell off the trail, but saved myself by grabbing at the jagged rock out-croppings so forcefully that several of my fingers started to bleed.

I misjudged the distance of the last step and landed at the bottom in a crouched position; the drop-off hadn't looked as great when viewed from above. The floor of the cove also covered more area than I expected. Although only a small patch of sand could be seen from up top, it actually extended back under the slanting walls of the old cave. The size of the open sand on the floor of the cove would vary with the tide, which came crashing through a large opening toward the west from the open sea. Visitors could also walk in from a small entrance on the north wall. I had done it myself in the past, but only at low tide. Care needed to be taken to not be hit by a wave and either dashed against the steep rocky sides of the cove or carried out to sea through the large opening. The water never receded from there, and it was really rough and choppy.

In my preoccupation with making a safe descent, I hadn't had time to look at the huge gray mass I had seen from above; now at the bottom, I turned toward it and noted, for the first time, a putrid smell. I immediately gagged. I got out my handkerchief and held it over my mouth and nose. That helped a little.

I came along the back of the mass. A fluke. Some barnacles. A sad, dead eye. My pulse was racing as I rounded the mass to view it head on—a whale had beached itself in this remote cove, and I was the first person on the scene!

God. What a rush. I had only seen whales from shore, never wanting to be part of the disturbance caused by tour boats going out to view them at close range. I could only marvel at the sheer size of this animal. I had read that Gray whales weigh as much as thirty-eight tons and grow as long as forty-five feet—as my reference material noted, five feet longer than a Greyhound bus. I felt like a midget standing next to it. But mixed with awe was a profound sadness. This whale didn't belong here, silent and still on the sand.

As a Gray, this was a baleen whale; instead of teeth, it had funny plates that it used to process food. It had probably become lost or sick on its way north and headed in here through the arched opening from the sea. Or maybe it had been attacked by sharks—chunks of flesh had been torn from its sides.

I rounded the body to view the whale from the front. It had rolled onto its side so that its massive jaw was agape. I stepped in closer to examine the long baleen plates. They were like tent poles supporting the top part of the mouth, arranged like the teeth in a comb. The bristles of the inner edge were woven together like a sieve to filter food from all the sea debris that ran through the whale's mouth as it swam. I touched the baleen, and it felt like what the reference books described: fingernails with bristles. A whole section of baleen had been hacked away, leaving a hole. Clumps of seaweed hung from the cavernous mouth.

I moved nearer as if I were viewing a display at the Museum of Natural History in New York. Although the whale had undoubtedly swum directly onto the shore before it died, the persistent tide had rolled it so that it was now facing northwest, as if the lifeless carcass was trying to head out to sea.

A ray of sun suddenly cast a direct light on the opening. I jumped back. Amid the strands of seaweed in the whale's mouth, I saw first an outstretched hand and, farther back, Howard Phelps's unseeing eyes looking back at me.

4

THE FIRST THING I DID was throw up, right there on the sand.

Not wanting to touch anything—and wanting to get out of there as fast as possible—I scrambled back up the path and ran home to call 911. I also called Susan, whose machine picked up after six unanswered rings. I left her a brief message about what I'd found. Then I walked back to Phelps's deck to wait. All hell would be breaking loose soon, and I knew the police would want to question me. I was right. Less than an hour later, the once-secluded cove was ablaze with floodlights and alive with police personnel and neighbors drawn to all the activity.

The local sheriff, Art Kutler, was first on the scene. He reminded me of a movie Gestapo agent with his brown shirt and pants. "Move over there, out of the way. What is your title? Mister Martindale or Doctor? You said you're with the university in Corvallis?" He kept up the questions before I could give answers. I hated being treated in such a condescending manner. He was making me feel like a suspect. My hackles rose.

"Tom Martindale will do fine, sheriff," I answered at last. "Yes, I teach on the main campus, but I'm on sabbatical to do some writing."

"Sabbatical. Is that where you people study some bullshit thing for several years at full pay while the rest of us have to work for a living?" He was really smirking over that one.

"You might say that," I said, adding to myself, if you were an ignorant county sheriff. But calling him names at this early stage of our acquaintanceship was probably not a good idea.

"You say you're a writer? You teach writing then?"

"Journalism. We throw a little reporting in with the writing."

"I've found what most reporters write is a lot of crap," he said.

My attempt at light humor wasn't getting me very far with this guy.

"How did you know the decedent?"

"I really didn't. We met this morning at the Marine Center, but only briefly. I discovered we were neighbors, and I just wanted to chat with him again."

"About what?"

The sheriff was really making me mad. I knew my answers were sounding apologetic and sputtery, but I couldn't seem to collect myself enough to make them sound any other way. "About nothing, really. We have a mutual friend."

"And that would be . . ."

"You wouldn't know her."

"But I may want to. Isn't that the point, professor?"

"Susan Foster. She's a marine biologist at the center. She and Phelps are teaching a seminar with me."

He wrote her name down on a pad.

"Did you attempt to break into the house here?"

"Of course not."

"You try to force the door?"

"No sheriff, I did not. I knocked on the front and when no one came, I walked around to the back. Then, I . . ."

"Good evening, Art. Or is it still afternoon?" A tall, well-groomed officer walked over to us. She looked in mock befuddlement at her watch, then smiled at both of us, as she introduced herself. "Angela Pride."

I stepped forward and we shook hands. I immediately liked her direct manner. She was polite and attentive and quite attractive. "Good to meet you. Tom Martindale." By her uniform and insignia, I could see that she was a sergeant in the Oregon State Police. My relief at having someone to deal with other than the obnoxious sheriff masked my surprise at finding a woman in such a senior position.

The dynamics changed with Sergeant Pride's arrival. She apparently had jurisdiction and quickly took over. Kutler glared at both of us, but soon jammed a cigar in his mouth and strolled back up the driveway to his car.

Sergeant Pride waited politely while I went over my story again. She may have been playing good cop to Kutler's bad cop, but the change in tone calmed me down immediately. Pride had me go over my story yet again, but waited politely until I finished to say anything herself. "Why don't we go down to the cove, and you walk me through everything that occurred?"

As we neared the edge of the yard, I suddenly remembered the cover page whose discovery had sent me down the hill in the first place. "Oh, I forgot something. I found this when I was looking for Phelps."

Holding it by the corner, she studied the sheet and its ominous dark stain. She reached into a pocket and pulled out a plastic bag, carefully placing the paper in it.

"I guess I didn't think about fingerprints."

She waved away my concerns and motioned me to follow her down the slippery path. My clothes were filthy by this time, so I paid less attention to the mud than on my first descent. I wondered about Sergeant Pride's immaculate uniform, but she arrived below without even a smudge. How did she do that?

When we got to the bottom, a pleasant looking man with a neatly trimmed beard and thick gray hair stepped forward. "Are you the officer in charge?" he asked Pride.

She nodded. "Angela Pride, Oregon State Police. You must be from the stranding network."

"Good to meet you. Jake McDowell." He turned to me.

"Tom Martindale. I found the body—bodies. You come out often for this kind of thing?"

"Yes, I do. I'm head of the Oregon Coast Stranding Network, and we get called every time a marine mammal is washed ashore, dead or alive. I work at the Marine Center, so I got this one. I'll be on hand until we figure out what happened to her and what to do with the carcass."

"So it's a female?" I asked. "Killed by sharks, I guess."

"No, killer whales," he replied, walking toward the carcass. "See these wounds? The flesh came off in chunks. Shark bites would be moon-shaped and much bigger. You would also see sideway slashes."

"Isn't it unusual for such a large whale to be killed by a smaller one?" asked the sergeant.

"No, not at all, especially at this time of year," said McDowell. "And it wasn't one Orca, it was a whole pod of them. You see, this is the time of year Gray whales migrate north to Alaskan waters. The mothers stick close to shore to protect and nurse their calves. By this point on the journey, they are very tired and low on fat and energy. Whalers called these females 'dry skins' and avoided hunting them because they had little oil."

"So a calf was probably trailing this whale? I asked. "Would it be cared for by other females in the pod?"

"Very unlikely," said McDowell. "It was probably killed when the mother was attacked."

Pride and I looked at the whale and both shook our heads at the thought. McDowell led us to the front of the carcass, where two men in biohazard suits were reaching in to pull out Phelps's body.

"Oh, and another thing you might find interesting," added McDowell. "This whale has no tongue. That's how the Orcas killed her—they pulled it out. It weighs a ton—I mean, quite literally, one ton. If the tongue was still in there, there wouldn't have been room for the body."

We contemplated the sad scene for a few more seconds.

"We'll let you get on with it," said Sergeant Pride.

We all shook hands.

"Good to meet you both," said McDowell with a smile.

"Me, too," I answered. "Good luck."

The sergeant gently touched my arm, and we started walking away from the carcass. I was about to gag again at the smell, but a gust of wind suddenly blew it away from my nostrils and I did not embarrass myself.

5

FRIDAY, APRIL 17

I WOKE UP TO MY ALARM going off at seven the next morning, lying on top of the bed still fully clothed. Everything smelled like dead whale—my bed, my clothes, my skin, my hair. The phone was ringing.

"Tom. Thank God you're okay."

"Morning, Susan. You got my message?"

"Yes, and it was all over the TV and radio this morning. Sorry you had to be the one to find him in such a gruesome way. Was the body really in the whale's mouth? How did he get? . . ."

"To tell you the truth, Sue, I don't really want to talk about it right now."

"Sorry. Do you feel like continuing the seminar and attending the conference?"

"It's still going forward?"

"The Powers That Be conferred and decided to go on. I mean, delegates are here from everywhere. There will be some kind of announcement."

"Seems kind of cold. . . . Sure. I'll be there as soon as I can get rid of this whale smell."

"Tomato juice works for skunks. I'm not sure about whales."

~ ~ ~

"Is this on?" John Strong, director of the center, was doing what first speakers at any podium invariably do: testing the microphone. Then, he continued the ritual by blowing directly into the device until it screeched. A technician kneeling at the side of the stage nodded his head vigorously, a slightly disgusted look on his face. I would have done the same thing had I been the speaker, although listening to this sound always irritate me. There are many of us in the world who do not like to deal with technical things. And the technical things—in seeming retaliation—fight back with their own policy of noncooperation.

"Good morning." Strong had gotten up his nerve and spoken. But he was standing too close and his voice boomed loudly over the speakers in the rather bleak auditorium of the center where we had gathered for the one-day symposium on whale population status. The sound was so loud, in fact, that several people milling around in the aisles turned abruptly, spilling their coffee in the process. The technician motioned for Strong to step back slightly. He did, pausing for a drink of water.

This might be a long day, I thought.

I had gotten press credentials because I planned to write an article on the politicization of whaling. The meeting might yield some interesting material for me. It also promised to be newsworthy because of the presence of officials of the International Whaling Commission (who opposed whale hunting of any kind) and delegations from Japan and the Alaska Eskimo Whaling Commission (both of which still hunted whales for food and opposed all efforts to stop killing them).

I was grateful that Susan Foster would be my guide through this maze of international intrigue and scientific jargon. She would also be a source because she was announcing what promised to be some fairly significant results from her research on whale population. Her figures would be used, at least in part, to set the quotas for the small amount of whale hunting that was still allowed for a few species.

"Welcome to the second annual symposium on whale population dynamics, sponsored by the university and the International Whaling Commission. Before we begin today's proceedings, I would like you all to stand for a moment of silence in honor of Dr. Howard Phelps, an extraordinary marine biologist at this center. As many of you know, Professor Phelps was found dead last night. After long and careful consideration, we decided to go forward with today's events because he would have wanted it that way. We dedicate this conference to Howard Phelps, an eminent scientist and avid conservationist." Strong bowed his head so abruptly that not everyone in the audience realized he had finished his remarks. As a result, some people were still getting up as others were sitting down. I wanted to snicker at the random up and down "wave," but the demand for decorum—given the solemn occasion—prevailed.

"Thank you. I know Professor Phelps would be touched by your gesture. Now, we'll begin our work. To start things off, I would like to introduce Harvey Martin, president of the university."

Martin, a tall, thin man who walked hunched over, came onto the stage from the wings to a smattering of applause. "Thank you, John. Minister Nagamo." He nodded toward the Japanese delegation, where the diminutive fisheries minister was barely visible beside the massive Mr. Jima until he stood up and bowed.

"Ambassador Riffstang." He glanced at a bunch of Nordic-looking men who rose and bowed as a group. Iceland. The other big whaling nation with a lot riding on the figures to be announced today.

"Sir Nigel." As in Parkhurst, the Englishman who headed the International Whaling Commission in London. He merely waved from a seated position.

"Distinguished colleagues, ladies and gentlemen. It has long been a goal of mine to host a major scientific conference at this center. And what better topic than one so vital to the salvation of this planet—the great, mysterious, mystical creatures we call whales."

My eyes started glazing over, but I forced myself to listen lest he say something I could use. He recounted the background to the university's whale research, who paid for it, where it was headed, etc. I actually found myself taking notes.

The president completed his remarks, then turned things over to Strong again. He, in turn, outlined the various sessions planned for the day. Although most of the interest was in Susan's whale numbers, there were also meetings on mating habits, nutrition, and history. Strong told us where we would have lunch, and then announced a half-hour break for coffee, sweet rolls, and rest room visits.

As I filed out with the twenty other reporters, I stopped by Susan, who was sitting near the back of the auditorium.

"Tom. How are you feeling?"

We embraced, and I was pleased that she didn't seem to recoil from me because of the way I smelled. The vinegar bath—and a generous application of Aramus aftershave—had apparently worked. I gave her a quick rundown of everything that had happened and mentioned finding the torn cover sheet, then asked her, "Did you wind up giving him what he wanted in your meeting yesterday?"

"Yeah. Strong asked me to. So Howard could go over the figures last night. He had calmed down and quit threatening me by that point. I was reluctant. I don't like to give in to bullying, but I didn't have much choice. If you found the cover, where is the report? Did his killer take it? God, my research certainly isn't anything to kill for. I'd like to find it, if it's around somewhere."

"I looked in his back door before I found the body, and there were no signs of a struggle or any papers. Maybe it's in his office. Could he have left it there? If the police haven't sealed it, we could have a look."

"They were around earlier looking in all the labs, but they didn't seem to be near his office. It's worth a try. I'd really like to get it. I don't want any of my results getting out until I've presented my figures later. I'll see if John has a key to Howard's office and if it's okay to go in. Would you go in with me as a . . . a witness?"

"Sure, Sue. Glad to."

Too bad things had come to this for her, that she thought she needed a witness when dealing with someone who had long been her mentor and friend. I shrugged and Sue walked away. She looked nice, having replaced the jeans and blue work shirt over turtleneck attire of yesterday with a navy-blue suit over silk blouse ensemble. Even her hair looked like it had been professionally done.

She joined Strong on the other side of the auditorium, who was talking to a group of people that included Minister Nagamo, Ambassador Riffstang, and Sir Nigel. He leaned over to hear as she whispered in his ear. He listened, nodded, looked over at me, then reached into his pocket to remove his key ring. He put on his glasses, then very meticulously searched the ring for, presumably, the master key that would open Howard Phelps's office door. When he found it, he removed it from the ring and gave it to Susan. He rejoined the group, and Sue walked back up the sloping aisle to me.

I followed her out into the lobby, then across to the staff hall that I had traversed the day before. We passed a door with Sue's name on it, then arrived at Phelps's office, where there was no sign of the police having been there. She opened the door and we went in.

The room was much more spacious than most faculty offices, as befitted the older man's status as a senior professor with tenure. It was also more orderly and better furnished than the norm. Phelps had purchased his own antique oak furniture and installed wall-to-wall carpeting. None of this was the usual gray steel with Formica top style issued by the State of Oregon to its employees. The walls were covered with framed prints of whales and sailing ships and diplomas and awards. His office was cozy and pleasant and even had a view of Yaquina Bay and the old section of Newport on the opposite shore.

Susan ignored all of these accoutrements and started immediately to look at things in the neat stacks of papers on his desk. "Looks like student papers, interoffice memos, scientific articles."

"What are we looking for?"

"It's about ten pages long with a cover sheet. The title is 'Current Whale Population Census.' It's on a blue cover with a university logo at the bottom. My name and title are there too, I think. Oh, I guess you already saw it. Maybe what we want doesn't even have a cover."

I moved to the Victorian stack bookcases that lined the room. The glass doors were closed on all of them, and no books seemed out of place. "Nothing on these shelves that I can see without moving books." I walked to the desk, as she slumped into one of the two chairs facing it, a dejected look on her face. "Do we dare look in these drawers?" I moved behind the desk and sat down in Phelps's swivel chair.

"Is it unlocked?"

I tried the main drawer over the kneehole. In these older models, its action often controlled the others. It slid open so quickly that all of its neatly arranged contents flew around inside. The long drawer contained pens, pencils, paper clips, and extra staples. The top side drawer held phone books and stationery. The two lower drawers were, in reality, one file drawer. Neatly labeled folders noted their predictable contents: "Department Memos," "College Procedures," "Promotion and Tenure," "Scientific Papers—Rough Drafts," and "Whale Population Conference Plans."

"This may be what we want."

I pulled that folder out and handed it to Susan, who grabbed it hopefully. She turned it sideways and began leafing through the contents. "This looks like rough drafts of letters of invitation, funding requests, a preliminary program. I guess Howard was on the organizing committee. My paper's not here. Damn."

Being basically nosy, I continued to look at the labels on the other folders. " 'Scott Szabo—Personal.' He's one of the graduate students in our seminar."

"Yes, he is." Her voice sounded odd, like she was holding something back, but the moment passed and she didn't say anything else. I kept thumbing through the other folders.

" 'Andy Kirk—Personal.' Who's Andy Kirk?"

"He was that graduate student who vanished last year after falling overboard from a Japanese whaling ship. He, Howard, and several other students spent a month as observers to see how humanely the Japanese slaughtered their whales. His body never turned up. The kid's family raised quite a stink, but the university and the Japanese government gave them a settlement. The terms were never disclosed."

As Susan spoke, I opened the folder and started to read what seemed to be a personal letter on top.

"Finding anything?" John Strong startled us both, as he pushed open the door.

I had just seen something so tantalizing that his interruption made me blush, like a kid caught red-handed. I closed the folder and put it back in its proper place. "Not a thing."

Susan rose from her chair, a movement that diverted Strong's eyes from me, as I slammed the file drawer. "The file for the conference had only committee things."

Strong looked aghast. "You're going through his files?"

"The drawer was unlocked. We thought a folder marked 'Whale Population Conference Plans' would be a likely place to find my paper." Both Susan and I had moved to the other side of the desk to face Strong, still standing in the doorway.

"Well, it bothers me. I was probably wrong to let you look in here. I think we'd better leave. The police will probably be securing this office. Do you have that key, Sue?"

She removed it from her pocket with some reluctance and handed it to her boss. He encompassed us both in a long sweep of his arm and hurried us from the room, locking the door in the process. "Poor Howard," he muttered.

As we walked down the hall to the auditorium, the first words of the letter came back to my mind: *Dr. P—You are more than a career mentor to me. You are my mentor in life and love . . .*

~ ~ ~

The rest of the day went fairly quickly. I met briefly with my students who were working on gathering information for their articles today; we would meet as a class tomorrow. I made sure I got back to the auditorium in time for Sue's presentation of her findings on whale population numbers. This would be the most interesting report today, in part because of the newsworthiness of what she had to say, but most of all because of the hostile way her message might be received.

In the fashion of scientific papers everywhere, she saved the best until last. She went over the statement of the problem and the methodology used to gather data before getting to the numbers everyone had come from thousands of miles to hear: just how many Bowhead whales and Minke whales are there in the world?

"My colleagues from various institutions in both the northern and southern hemispheres have collated the number of sightings and extrapolated from that data the number of whales in two species: *Balaenoptera acutorostrata*, known as the Minke whale, and *Balaena mysticetus*, the Bowhead whale. We recognize the economic and cultural implications of our findings. We did not take our task lightly. Our findings are as follows."

There was a distinct air of anticipation in the room, the audience suddenly becoming very quiet.

"For *Balaenoptera acutorostrata*, the Minke whale, the number of species in Antarctica is four hundred thousand—a drop of fifty-two percent from earlier in this century."

Ambassador Riffstang was red in the face. Minister Nagamo's face was impassive, but the hulking Mr. Jima was glowering. The IWC permitted the Japanese to hunt Minke whales based on a certain percentage of the total count over a two-year period. Susan's figure was less than they had hoped for. They might have to cancel their annual hunt.

"For *Balaena mysticetus*, the Bowhead whale, the number of species in Western Arctic waters is two thousand five hundred—a drop of twenty-five percent from initial stock size earlier in the century."

Although neither Strong nor the president had singled them out, five men and a woman, who were sitting together on the side, appeared to be Eskimos. If population figures were too low, they wouldn't be able to hunt Bowhead whales, which they consider a vital part of their culture. Now it was their turn to glower and frown. One of the men in the delegation slammed his fist into the seat in front of him and shouted "Shit."

Susan paused to sip from a glass of water and, no doubt, catch her breath. She was ignoring the various reactions her words had evoked. "In closing, I wish to thank my colleagues at the other universities, and our spotters in aircraft and on shore, whose names are too numerous to mention here, but which are listed at the end of my paper. My university colleague Howard Phelps helped me considerably. We all feel his loss. Also, I would be remiss if I did not publicly thank our funding sources, which include the National Oceanic and Atmospheric Administration, the United States Navy, the National Science Foundation, and the J. R. Higgins Charitable Trust. We hope you will find the data useful in charting the future course of whale management, both of these two species and all others under the care of the International Whaling Commission. I would be happy to answer any questions."

"My dear Professor Foster . . ." Ambassador Riffstang was first on his feet and walked to one of the many microphones situated around the auditorium. Iceland professed to kill Minke whales only to conduct what it called "scientific research" on their carcasses, but many people suspected this was a subterfuge. What they were really doing was killing whales in order to sell the meat to Japan. "I must respectfully challenge your data on the Minke whale. Our scientists have done their own census and found there to be, in our waters alone, ten to fifteen percent more whales than your figures show. What do you say to that?"

"I guess I would have to question the veracity of your find-ings, given what has been riding on the result." Even a casual bystander like me knew that Susan probably should not have been so blunt, especially with an ambassador. She must really be edgy and angry at how this session was going. "I mean everyone knows that your country . . ."

"I think what Professor Foster meant to say is that honest people differ on many issues, not the least of which is how many whales exist in the world." Director Strong strode briskly from the wings to Susan's side to take charge of the proceed-ings. He gently nudged Susan away from the podium, and she stepped back.

"I must respectfully agree with my distinguished colleague from Iceland." Now it was Minister Nagamo's turn to enter the discussion. He bowed to Susan before starting to eviscerate her in front of the assembled scientists and reporters in his impec-cable English. "If you will permit me, ladies and gentlemen." He had turned to face the entire room, pointedly turning his back on Susan and the nervous-looking John Strong. "Never in all my years as a scientist have I encountered such a flawed piece of research as that presented today by Professor Foster."

Susan seemed to sink at his words. She stared at the floor and said nothing. Director Strong was equally mute.

"My government will oppose the use of this data to set whale harvesting quotas at the International Whaling Commission meeting in Buenos Aires this June. I will issue a detailed response to her report tomorrow. My staff is waiting for substantiating material from Tokyo." He sat down.

"We protest the blatant racism inherent in this white woman's figures." One of the Eskimos was standing now. He was tall and had long, black hair hanging loosely to his shoul-ders. He—and the others in the delegation from the Alaska

Eskimo Whaling Commission—were well dressed in pin-striped suits. Incongruous to that formal attire, they were also wearing a lot of ivory jewelry—bracelets, rings, and headbands.

"Excuse me, sir. Would you identify yourself?" Strong was trying to deflect the man's loud protest.

"I am Damon Istook, chairman of the Alaska Eskimo Whaling Commission. May I go on?"

Strong nodded curtly. "But please don't get personal."

"As I was saying, what can a white person know of our suffering over the centuries and our cultural need to hunt Bowhead whales? If we cannot do this, we will die as a people. We protest the falsity of these numbers."

The rhetoric was really flowing—at the expense of Susan and the whales. I felt sorry for her. All the color was gone from her face, and she stood to the side of the podium, looking defeated. She seemed to have lost the desire to fight.

"This seems like a good time to take our afternoon coffee break." The always expedient John Strong had finally ended Susan's torment. "We will reconvene in this room at three P.M. for a session on whale num . . ." Strong stopped in mid-sentence. In all the hubbub, I failed to notice Sheriff Kutler and two deputies standing in the wings, just off stage. They now moved toward Susan.

"Susan Foster. I have a warrant for your arrest for the murder of Howard Phelps. You have the right to remain silent. Anything you say can be used against you in court. You have the right to talk to a lawyer and have him present while you are being questioned. If you cannot afford a lawyer . . ."

6

THE ROOM WAS IN AN UPROAR. It seemed like everyone had surged toward the front of the auditorium. I couldn't get near the stage exit where Susan had disappeared, so I ran up the aisle and out the door into the aquarium area of the center. As usual, tourists were milling about looking at the various exhibits—oblivious to what was going on just a few feet away. Out front of the building, there were no police cars in the parking lot, so I walked around to the back. There two sheriff's cars were parked close to a rear door. Susan, in handcuffs, was just being led to the second car by a female deputy.

"Sue, Sue! Are you all right?"

"Not so fast, buddy." A deputy stepped in front of me, hand on holstered gun.

"I need to speak to her."

"Okay, Troy, let him through." Sheriff Kutler had appeared at Susan's side. "This your girlfriend, Einstein?"

"We're friends, yes."

"Friend or not, this doesn't concern you. She can talk to an attorney—that's it. This doesn't involve you. At least, I don't think so at this time. If you want to stay out of trouble yourself, get out of here. Troy, escort our esteemed professor out of the area."

"Talk to my secretary," Sue shouted to me. I turned as she ducked her head into the car. The female deputy was holding her hand over Sue's head to keep it from hitting the roof. I could only stand and watch helplessly as both cars sped away.

I walked back inside to Susan's office. It had already been sealed with yellow police tape.

"Oh, there you are, Mr. Martindale." It was Mildred, Susan's secretary, and she was crying. "It's so awful. I know she couldn't have done what they say she's done. There's just no way. The lady deputy told me they've taken her to the courthouse. I've called her attorney. He's going to meet her there. Oh, and she wanted me to give you her passkey. She said you'd know what to do with it."

~ ~ ~

No one would tell me anything about Susan when I got to the courthouse. I went to the district attorney's office, then to the court clerk. If I wasn't getting the official runaround, you could have fooled me. I stepped out into the hall to contemplate my next move and found it full of people: average citizens reporting for jury duty, attorneys, inmates being led to courtrooms by deputies. I was startled by the confusion.

Out of this chaotic scene stepped Angela Pride. "Oh, Mr. Martindale. I'm sorry to tell you that a colleague of yours, . . ." she consulted a slip of paper in her hand, ". . . a Ms. Susan Foster, has been arrested for the murder of Howard Phelps."

"Yes, I know. I was there when the sheriff came for her. Tell me, why did he have to do it in such a public way? She was more humiliated than was necessary, don't you think?"

Sergeant Pride looked around before she answered. "Yes, I agree. I thought the sheriff agreed to let me do the arrest in her office later, but he went ahead. I think Art resents being outranked by a woman. Also, he likes to put on a show, now and again."

"That's putting it mildly. Why the urgency?"

"We found the rest of that whale report and a ball-peen hammer with blood on it in her lab. That was all we needed to pick her up."

"Can I see her?"

"Not until she's arraigned tomorrow. She's called a criminal attorney. Her local guy only does civil stuff, I guess."

As I drove back to the center, I debated about whether I should get involved. Sure, Sue and I had been friends a long time. But part of me still resented what she had said about me. Even if you made allowances for her being drunk at the time, that was a very hurtful thing to say.

But that was about me. Right now, with what she was facing—arrest, possible indictment for murder, a difficult trial— her well-being was more important than my wounded pride. Despite our failed relationship, I wanted to help her. Also, I felt certain that no argument over whale population data or even concerns over her pending promotion would lead her to commit murder. And if Sue hadn't killed Phelps, who had? I felt my investigative reporter instincts kick into gear.

I parked in front of the center and noticed that the demonstrators I had seen the day before were picketing in front of the main entrance. Usually these protests were orderly, although a few years ago, someone had thrown blood on members of the Japanese delegation as they walked into a meeting in Bournemouth, England. The small nature of this IWC conference and the fact that it was being held in a relatively remote location meant that only a few protesters had shown up.

The members of the group had completed the signs I had only glimpsed before; some of them were inflammatory and racist.

"Save the Whales"

"End Slaughter of Innocent Whales"

"Whale Blood on Jap Hands! Nuke the Japs!"

"Boycott All Icelandic Products"

"Send Eskimo Whalers Back to Siberia"

The men and women were dressed like Hollywood's idea of what radical "enviroconservationists" should look like: jeans, blue work shirts, parkas, and boots. On closer look, however, I could see that the clothes were clean, new, and brand name: L. L. Bean, Orvis, and Timberland. Two people in the center of the shouting throng looked familiar as I got closer: a small woman with delicate features and a lot of dark, curly hair hovered over by a very large man. It was Mara and Trog from the seminar. I nodded as I passed them, but she ignored me and kept yelling at the top of her lungs.

I neared the door at the same time two Japanese women from the delegation were entering. Probably translators. As we walked through, Mara ducked from behind the rope barricade and spit in the face of the older woman. Because I had stepped back to open the door for them, the second hail of spittle missed me, landing on the other side of the glass at about eye level. The Japanese women were horrified, as was I. Mara whooped with victory as she was led away by police, her protector following meekly behind.

Once inside, I offered the Japanese women my handkerchief and bowed, withdrawing as quickly as I could to the staff area. I headed toward the director's office. Strong was standing in the hall, talking with the ambassador from Iceland. They parted as I approached.

"Dr. Strong. I just came from trying to see Susan. They wouldn't let me near her."

"The whole thing's awful. Poor old Phelps, too, as I said this morning."

"I suppose the university will help defend her."

"We can't use taxpayer's money for a murder defense."

"I know the college can't pay for an attorney. I mean to protect her reputation. To vouch for her character. That kind of thing."

"We'd better see how it all plays out, don't you think? I'm convening a short meeting of the conference at five. Some new data turned up—you'll probably want to hear about it. Just come to the auditorium."

He hurried off before I could ask any questions. From his earlier answer, Strong seemed to be letting Susan get through this on her own. People like Strong should be supporting her, but they were apparently going to run the other way. "Academics," I muttered to myself.

I pushed through the "Staff Only" door and walked to her office. I wanted to try the door, but felt intimidated by the yellow police tape. Her lab, at the inner core of the building, had a similar barrier. I couldn't go in—at least not in broad daylight. And if I got in, what was I looking for? The police had already taken their most incriminating evidence. Walking back, I passed Phelps's closed office. Oddly, no crime scene tape guarded his door.

I spent the hour or so until the conference reconvened by reading and photocopying background material on whales to use in the seminar tomorrow. Although I had been interested in whales for a long time, I didn't know much about them. My journalistic instincts told me that readers would be as fascinated as I was about these gigantic but gentle creatures. The students would love writing about them, too.

~   ~   ~

"Thank you for coming back in on such short notice."

Because the conference had officially adjourned, John Strong was addressing a group about half the size of the one assembled earlier in the day. All the important players were there, however: the Japanese, Icelanders, Eskimos, and Sir Nigel of the IWC. The media people were still around, too—the print reporters sitting in one section near the front, the TV crews shining their lights on the podium and milling around on the side.

"I mentioned this morning the news of the untimely death of Professor Howard Phelps, a pioneer marine biologist and long-time colleague at the center. In looking through some of his effects earlier this afternoon, I discovered an updated report with whale population figures that are significantly different from those presented to you earlier today. Given Dr. Phelps's reputation, I have decided to make this report the official document of this conference and our final word on whale population numbers."

Strong was hanging Susan out to dry. He wasn't mentioning her name or noting her arrest, but he was trashing her figures without a second thought. At a signal from Strong, secretaries walked down the aisle from the back of the auditorium and handed out copies of something called "Current Whale Population Census—Revised." Immediately, all the principal players turned to the section containing numbers. Just as quickly, they began to smile—all except Sir Nigel who, as head of the IWC, had to remain neutral.

"Given the need for many of you to get to the airport, I don't plan to go over the report in any depth—only the numbers listed on page fourteen and page twenty-five, the Bowhead and Minke sections, have changed. Because they represent amounts twenty percent greater than yesterday's reported totals, our marine mammal research unit here at the center is prepared to recommend to the International Whaling Commission that all previous hunting permits be continued indefinitely for those nations wishing to harvest whales for scientific and cultural reasons. With that, we stand adjourned."

"Dr. Strong. Dr. Strong!" I seldom ask questions or talk at all in a group of strangers, but I was on my feet before Strong finished talking.

"I'm sorry, Mr. Martindale, but we haven't the time for questions."

The group seemed content with Strong's decision and was getting up to leave. The din in the room grew louder. No one paid any attention to me. I sat down and looked more closely at the report. Strong was right: the totals for Bowheads and Minkes were twenty percent higher than Susan's figures. Where did this come from? There had been no report in Phelps's office the day before. Was he killed because the report was written or because he tried to change its conclusions? Was what we were looking at a concoction by Phelps's killer?

And, was that killer one of the men in the room gazing gleefully at the new report? Come to think of it, Minister Nagamo, Ambassador Riffstang, and the Eskimo Istook had rarely looked happier. I walked out of the auditorium in total disgust.

7

I RETURNED TO THE CENTER AT TEN P.M. using Susan's key to enter by the rear door. I would use my faculty card as ID if anyone challenged me. The police tape across Susan's office and lab doors still daunted me, but I was aiming at a bigger target anyway.

Miraculously, the door of Howard Phelps's office still had no tape across it. Even better, it was open. No one was inside, but a janitor's cart was parked nearby; the office was being cleaned. I could hear a radio blaring country music farther down the hall. I decided to find a hiding place in the office and wait quietly until the janitor finished and moved on.

I didn't have long to wait. In about ten minutes, I heard footsteps on the polished floor. Soon, a head of tightly curled gray hair appeared in the doorway. The janitor, a short plump woman wearing a smock and carrying a feather duster, seemed to be taking a last look at her handiwork. I could only see part of her from my hiding place in a big oak cupboard.

"Okay. That finishes you up," she said to the room as she switched off the light and disappeared, closing the door.

I let out my breath slowly, but stayed put. The sound of her shoes grew gradually quieter as she continued working down the hall. Soon the music got dimmer. She was probably in the other wing by now, so I climbed out of the cupboard. Then I closed the blinds and put on the rubber gloves that I had brought with me. Melodrama aside, I didn't want to take the chance of my fingerprints being found here on any later police search. Then I turned on a small penlight.

I didn't expect to find anything dealing with the revised whale report. After thinking about it all afternoon, I was convinced that whoever had revised it had done so elsewhere and deposited their work here for Strong to find. He seemed too guileless to be part of anything this bad. And they must have known him well enough to realize that he would jump at the chance to ease tensions and accept the new report without hesitation. That way, he could end his conference with everybody happy—no matter what that did to Susan.

I had wanted to point all of this out to him, but was told that he had left immediately to drive with Sir Nigel in a limousine to the Portland International Airport, over two hours away.

No, I knew no remnant of the report would be found here. Instead, I was interested in that file folder I'd seen yesterday in Phelps's drawer, the one marked "Andy Kirk—Personal." It was still there.

The folder appeared to contain letters between Phelps and Kirk. Susan had said that Kirk was one of the professor's graduate students. The meticulous professor had arranged everything in reverse chronological order. The letter I'd seen before was on top. On the bottom was a copy of the letter Phelps had sent to Kirk two years before, asking him to join his research team. It noted his duties, pay, and the waiving of his tuition. Clipped to that was Kirk's somewhat breathless acceptance. Kirk's grade slips were included, too. He had been an honor student in biology at a Portland high school, then at the university itself, where Phelps had apparently heard about his work in marine biology.

Interspersed among the official papers were a series of personal letters that led me to believe that Phelps and Kirk had become lovers a year after first meeting. It was hard to tell how things had gotten started, but the intensity of the relationship—at least on Kirk's part—was apparent from even a casual glance. Phrases like *I'll never forget last night* and *I never want to leave your side* don't leave much to the imagination. The letter I read yesterday—the one on top—had talked about *my mentor in life and love.*

Good grief. Phelps was playing with dynamite here. Any kind of sexual relationship between professor and student can end even a tenured faculty member's career in a hurry. I think the phrase is "moral turpitude." Odd for Phelps to let himself get involved like this, with all the risks in that kind of behavior. Being meticulous in his paperwork apparently didn't translate to meticulousness in his morals. Odd, too, that he kept this stuff here in the office. He must have felt invulnerable.

Taped to the inside of the folder was a newspaper clipping, dated a year ago.

Marine biology student feared lost at sea

Andrew M. Kirk, 22, of Portland, a graduate student in the marine biology program in Newport, was apparently swept overboard early Thursday from a Japanese whaling research vessel one hundred miles west of the Oregon coast.

Kirk, his professor Howard Phelps, three other students, and another marine biologist were spending a week on board the Setsu Yama studying Japanese whaling techniques and research.

Phelps told authorities that Kirk had gone out on deck in the middle of the night after feeling nauseated because of rough seas. When he didn't return after an hour, his cabin mate, Scott Szabo of Malibu, California, became alarmed and informed Phelps, who notified the ship's captain.

Small boats from the ship, joined later by a U.S. Coast Guard helicopter, searched the area around the ship and its

*previous location for five hours before giving up. A Coast
Guard spokesman in Newport said that an investigation
would be forthcoming.*

I'll be damned. So Scott Szabo, one of the students in my
seminar, had been on the ship when Andy Kirk fell overboard—along with another professor. I'd have to ask Sue who
it was and talk to him.

I jotted down the date of the clipping. Someone would likely
have a copy of the report the Coast Guard was certain to have
conducted. I vaguely remembered the incident, but I don't
remember much coming of it. Was the college able to hush up
the findings? How did Kirk's family react? Sue said they got a settlement. I recalled the shouting match I had overheard outside
Phelps's office. The other man had to have been Kirk's father.

All grade sheets are sent to a student's home address, not the
school address. I copied down an address in Portland's fashionable West Hills. Kirk must have come from money. I had
been so intent on the clipping that I hadn't looked at the photo
printed with it. It was a mug shot of a good-looking young
man dressed in a coat and tie. He had dark hair and a nice
smile. I closed the folder and put it back in the drawer.

Then I remembered the other file I had seen the day
before—the one marked "Scott Szabo—Personal." At first I
couldn't locate it. Maybe someone had removed it. Then I
found it behind a binder marked "Faculty Senate." I guess I had
gotten it out of order in my haste earlier in the day to cram
everything back into the drawer when Strong walked in on us.
I pulled it out and opened it flat on the desk top.

Like Kirk's, this dossier recorded another of Phelps's relation-
ships with a student. The grade slips and original letter of acceptance were there, along with a few handwritten notes and letters.

One read *I've been an admirer of you for years. I was hoping you would take me under your wing and help me with my career in marine biology.* That was almost word for word what Szabo had said to me yesterday when we met in class. His approach was apparently the same with every professor he thought might help him.

Other notes and letters dealt mainly with Szabo's career plans and requests for help in applying for fellowships. Most had Phelps's recommendations stapled to them. Included in the same sheaf of papers was an envelope with "Dr. P" written on the outside.

Obviously, this was a bit juicier because Phelps hadn't kept it flattened out with the other letters. I hesitated for only a second about taking it out; holding the penlight in my mouth, I pulled the folded letter from the unsealed envelope.

It was Szabo's official rejection from a marine biology institute in New Zealand. He had applied for a one-year research fellowship and was being turned down because of a low rating from his major professor—Phelps. Szabo had apparently given the letter to Phelps, with the added handwritten notation: *How can you ruin my life after all we've meant to each other?* Another message had been written in below Szabo's, probably by Phelps: *I couldn't let you go, Scotty. I need you.*

I checked the date: three weeks ago. So Phelps and Szabo had had their flare-up recently. And, even more interestingly, it seemed that Phelps had picked Szabo to fill Andy Kirk's role— in both the lab and possibly his life. I put the folder back behind that of the missing Kirk.

What else would this desk yield? I spied an old metal box in the back of the bottom left drawer, partially covered with blank paper and envelopes. It was locked, but didn't look all that formidable. The latch easily gave way to the force of the letter opener. Inside were more papers, grouped by year and held together with rubber bands. The most recent year—last year, actually—was on top. Phelps's habits were consistent.

I unfolded the stack labeled "1991": bank draft records of some sort, plus deposit records. *Payment to Howard Phelps, Ph.D., from Hirakawa Research Fund, Tokyo, Japan. For technical assistance in whale research, the sum of $50,000 will be paid annually.*

So Phelps was being paid from some kind of Japanese research fund to do whale research. How could that possibly be ethical? How did he keep these payments quiet? Did Susan know? That might explain how he got permission to observe activities on board a Japanese whaling ship. I'd read in my research that these ships are usually closed to outsiders.

Suddenly I heard a sound outside the window. A guard? The police? I quickly switched off my penlight and rewrapped the papers in the dark. As I extended a rubber band over the bulky pile, it broke.

"Damn."

No time to look for a replacement. I felt for—and found—the box and stuffed the papers inside as quietly as I could. I put the box back in its place in the rear of the drawer and slid it closed. The lock was obviously jimmied, but I had bigger worries now.

The chair squeaked as I moved it back from the desk to get up. I froze, my heart beating so hard I could hear it reverberating in my ears. I got up and eased myself toward the window. There seemed to be loud whispering going on outside—in Japanese. I lifted the lowest wooden blind a fraction. At first I couldn't see anything outside except the twinkling lights of the old bay-front section of Newport across Yaquina Bay. After my eyes got used to the dark, I could see two men crouched down a few feet out from the building.

At about the same moment, one of the men got up. It was Mr. Jima, the Japanese bodyguard. I guess breaking and entering was part of his job description. He was standing next to me by this time, only a pane of glass and the partially closed blinds separating us. I sucked in my breath and slipped back a bit. I don't think he saw me because by this time he was attaching something to the glass above the latch; it was some kind of suction cup. This done, he began to use a glass cutter to make a circle. He was planning to open the window and come in.

There should be plenty of time for me to get out, but at that moment, the country music from the janitor's radio suddenly got louder—not loud enough so Jima could hear, but loud enough for me to know that she was just down the hall.

I was trapped between the two of them. I didn't relish a scuffle with him. Even in the dark, I was at a disadvantage. He probably outweighed me by seventy-five pounds. But I would just as soon not let her see me either—all that awkward explaining.

As the glass cutting got louder and the music more intense, I pondered my alternatives.

In my mind, there wasn't much choice. I could hide out in the cupboard and wait for this Japanese goon to complete his break-in or I could try to get out the door and deal with the janitor. That wasn't much of a decision.

I opened the door as quietly as I could and slipped out into the hall. I was in luck. The janitor had moved to the small lab across the hall and just gone inside, where I could hear her emptying wastebaskets. The music's loud blare was muffling both Mr. Jima's felonious activities and my hastily departing footsteps.

Country roads, take me home, to the place I belong.

8

SERGEANT PRIDE PULLED SOME STRINGS so I could visit Susan in jail early the next morning. Sue looked tired and worried as she was led into the small room where I had been told lawyers usually conferred with clients.

"Hi, Sue. How are you?"

"No touching of any kind." The matron, a rather stout woman in a brown uniform, pointed at a sign on the far wall, anticipating what I wanted to do—hold Sue as tightly as I could. Her remark caused me to raise my arms and step back, as if I'd just touched something hot. Sue seemed so numb because of what was happening to her that she didn't react at all. She stood there with her shoulders hunched and looked blankly at me.

The matron left the room to take up a post just outside the now closed door. Every once in a while she would look in, I guess to make sure I didn't have a lock pick hidden in my coat sleeve.

"I'm okay, just really tired."

Susan slumped in a plastic chair on one side of the table. I sat down opposite her.

"Do you need anything? Toothbrush, comb?"

"Do I look that bad?" She smoothed her hair with one hand.

"No, no. I didn't mean that. I was just thinking of something to help you."

"It'll take more than a toothbrush and a comb, I'm afraid. They say I killed Howard. They found that other copy of my report and a hammer on the floor of my lab. What a stupid way to think! If I was conniving enough to kill him, why would I be so careless as to drop the two most crucial pieces of evidence?"

"Sheriff Kutler is not all that bright. But there's more bad news, I'm afraid. John Strong found a copy of a revised report on population figures in Phelps's office."

The look on her face was of complete surprise. "That's impossible. There was no revised report."

"Naturally, it shows higher numbers for Bowheads and Minkes, so everyone is pleased. They're all leaving the conference with a mandate to continue killing whales. It's pretty obvious that someone with a vested interest in whaling concocted the new report."

"Did Strong go along with that?"

"He didn't bat an eye. He passed copies out, took no questions, and adjourned the meeting. Before I could talk to him, he was off to the Portland airport with Sir Nigel."

"God. Doesn't anyone care about being honest?"

"Apparently not. I think I know the answer to another question, but I want to get it straight in my mind. Why did people from all the various sides of this issue go after you with such vehemence yesterday?"

"A lot is at stake. The Japanese want the whale meat for consumers. The Icelanders are making money supplying them. The Eskimos don't want the white man to rob them of another part of their culture. I threatened all three in different ways. I knew they'd be angry, but I didn't expect these personal attacks. I worked so hard on this—checking and rechecking. Talking to spotters. Coordinating logistics. Raising money. It isn't like I made it all up. I wanted it to be right. And then there's my impending promotion and tenure. This will screw that up in a big way. The academic world hates anyone who makes waves. It's all so uncivilized to most academics. They'd rather have you just keep quiet. The old stiff upper lip."

"Is that why no one came to your defense?"

"What I call the academic mind is hard to figure out sometimes. People save themselves when things get sticky. They watch out for themselves above all. If helping someone in trouble might cast any negative light on them, they do all they can to distance themselves. Even the people who wish you well, don't wish you too well, I'm afraid."

"So I've noticed. Sue, there's something else. I've been nosing around a little. Did you know that Phelps had been getting money from a Japanese research foundation for five years or so?"

"God, no. Nothing like that ever came up. He always talked about what he called private money, but I assumed it was from his family or something. He's always had a trust fund. How did you find out?"

I dropped my voice to a whisper. This was, after all, the sheriff's jail. I doubted that the room was bugged, but our voices were echoing even when we talked in a normal tone. "Let's just say I found out in my own way. It's best if you don't know how. Trust me on this—I've seen the records. But how could he get money like that and not go through the normal research office at the university?"

"There's no way, unless he just opened a bank account somewhere and wrote checks on it himself. That would be very much against the rules. He'd have been strung up if Strong or the dean ever found out."

"Also, do you think Howard Phelps was gay? And did he have an affair with Andy Kirk?"

"There were rumors about it—and some jokes—but I never saw anything. Kirk was a nice kid, but never one of our top students. He hadn't done as well in graduate school as he had as an undergraduate. Some people were surprised that Howard asked someone with that kind of so-so record to attend the scientific exchange on the Japanese ship. You know about that?"

I nodded.

"Oh, yeah. I guess I told you yesterday."

"That graduate student in our seminar—Scott Szabo? He was on the trip, too. I read that in the newspaper clipping about Andy Kirk's disappearance."

"Yes, he was there. What does that have to do with anything?" She seemed suddenly uneasy about talking about Szabo.

"Oh, maybe nothing, really. I was just surprised to find his name in the story. And another thing . . ." I leaned in close so I could lower my voice, "It seems that Scott Szabo became Phelps's special student after Kirk disappeared. I mean special in the lab and between the sheets."

A look of horror spread across her face. "Scott and Howard? No, I don't believe it! Scott's older, not an impressionable kid like Andy Kirk. He's always struck me as very heterosexual. I mean I've seen him with girls, I think."

"Well, I saw what I saw in the file. There was a certain tone to the notes they exchanged. I wouldn't be surprised to find that Szabo initiated things. In the few times I've talked to him, he struck me as someone who would do anything for a good grade, anything to advance his career."

She jumped to her feet quickly, knocking over the chair. "You're wrong, Tom! What would you know about it anyway?"

Sue started rubbing her temples. "God. Why did I say that? I'm sorry, Tom. I shouldn't have said it."

"Don't worry about it," I said, waving my hand as if it would wipe away her words."

"I'm sorry," she said again, seeming to be on the verge of tears. "I'm really beat. Getting a headache. I never have headaches!" She started to sit down, then lost her footing, and knocked over another chair in the process. The clatter attracted the attention of the guard, who walked back into the room and stood by the door, clanking her keys. I quickly put the chairs in order.

"You were asking about the students on the trip," she said, "to return to more mundane matters. Anyway, the trip was a big deal for the students. I suppose some of the kids resented the fact that Howard chose Kirk to go instead of them. But after he was lost at sea, that got all of the attention and nothing else was ever said."

I decided to drop the subject of Scott Szabo for now.

"Was there a connection between receiving permission to go on that trip and the money he got all those years?"

"It seems so now, but of course no one knew about those funds before."

"Time's up, mister. You'll have to go," said the matron, impatiently.

"Thanks for everything, Tom. I'm sorry for losing my temper."

"It's okay, Sue. Forget about it."

"You'll have to go, mister." The matron was back, standing just inside the door, clanking her key ring.

"Oh, one more thing: how did that paper get in your lab if you didn't put it there?"

"I don't know. I hadn't been in my lab for a few days because I was so busy with the conference."

"You've got an attorney. Is he any good?"

"She comes very highly recommended. A criminal attorney from Eugene. I was denied bail and I'm to be arraigned later today. I guess they'll go to the grand jury for an indictment a few days from now."

"I'll try to see you as often as I can. Stay well—and try to be optimistic."

Her voice, mumbling thanks, trailed off as the matron led her out of the room. She looked about ten years older than she had yesterday. After she disappeared through the steel door, I remembered that I had forgotten to ask her the name of the other marine biologist who had been on board the ship. I'd have to remember to inquire about that when I saw her again.

As I came out of the main jail door downstairs, Sheriff Kutler was walking toward me on the path to the parking lot, the usual insipid grin on his face.

"Trying to get in to see your girlfriend? I hope you haven't been bothering our most famous inmate, Professor Martindale."

"I did more than try, sheriff. I've just been talking with her."

The sheriff's face got beet red almost immediately. He started to sputter. "God damn jail staff. I left strict orders she was to have no visitors but her attorney. You an attorney, Martindale?"

I shook my head.

"Then you lied to get in."

"I didn't say anything about my status, sheriff. I presented my name at the main desk and I got in." I was backing away from the bulky form in front of me. "Have a good day."

I turned and started walking toward the parking lot, hoping that an alarm wouldn't sound or that I wouldn't be surrounded by helmeted deputies carrying mace and holding back snarling German shepherds straining to get a bite out of me.

"God damn Pride. She got you in. You've just seen your girl-friend for the last time in this jail. I hope you kissed her goodbye."

"The matron said no touching, so we didn't. I could go back in and give it another try, I guess." The sheriff was still fuming as I walked away. I quickly started my car and drove out of the parking lot.

It was a clear spring morning, and the sun was already up above the trees to the west of town. Its rays made the water sparkle as I drove my car across the Yaquina Bay Bridge. Below, to the left, I could catch glimpses of the Marine Center through gaps in the bridge railing. I looked to my right in time to see a fishing boat sail around the jetty, heading north. If its owner was planning to catch many fish this day, he was getting a late start. It was nearly nine thirty and the rest of the fleet had sailed hours ago.

I turned off the highway onto a side road. After making a series of right turns, I passed the old mobile home that was surrounded by pieces of driftwood of all shapes and sizes, many resembling various sea creatures. As a result, the owner called his place Zig Zag Zoo. In this area of modest homes, it was common for people to hang the driftwood and Japanese glass floats that washed ashore outside their houses. Although some of my academic colleagues considered this somewhat declassé, I found it quaint and charming. It was as much a part of the Oregon coast to me as the unmistakable smell of the sea that brings pleasant thoughts to mind—of walking on the beach, building sand castles, hearing gulls caw in the distance.

Five minutes and more right turns, and I was in the parking lot of the center. The class was convening at the end near the area where seawater from the bay was pumped into a maze of pipes for use in experiments in the various labs. I would be giving the students their writing assignments; Randy Wells would be handing out tasks for those interested in taking photographs. The students would have two weeks to do the work on their own; we would reconvene after that to critique what they had done.

Randy was already walking along the sandy beach of the bay as I strolled over from my car.

"Morning, Tom."

"Hi, Randy. You're already shooting?"

"Yeah. I've been out here since first light. I love the effect those early, weaker rays have on the water. See those gulls across the bay?"

I shielded my eyes with one hand and nodded in the general direction of his gesture.

"I used a telephoto lens to get some good shots—probably got thirty good ones. With these motor drive cameras, you can shoot a lot of film fast. If one frame doesn't measure up, one of the next twenty-nine probably will. Photographers call that insurance. Film is cheap, so you might as well use it to your advantage."

"I see what you mean. In my family, in the old Kodak Brownie days, you took one shot and that was it."

"Professor Martindale. Can I talk to you for a minute—in private?" Scott Szabo had walked up behind us so quietly, I jumped when I heard my name.

"God, Scott. You startled me. Sure, let's step over there by the pumping station. I guess we'll start in ten minutes or so, Randy."

Scott was dressed in shorts and a tank top. We talked as we walked.

"You may wish you had warmer clothes by the time the day is over," I said, glancing at his cold-looking legs and bare feet.

"I grew up in Southern California. I surfed a lot and got used to not wearing much. I always forget that Oregon isn't like that. It is much colder here. I've got pants, a jacket, and shoes in my car."

"You'll be glad you have them."

We reached the pump house, and I turned to face him. "Is this private enough for you? What did you want to talk about?"

"I just wanted to tell you again how pleased I am to finally meet you and take a class from you. I'd really like us to be friends. We're not all that far apart in age, and I'd like us to get to know each other socially. So, I was wondering if you'd care to have dinner with me tonight, my treat?"

Boy, this guy didn't beat around the bush when it came to working on his grade point average.

"That's very thoughtful, Scott. I appreciate the invitation, but I have to be frank with you. I've always made it a point not to socialize with my students, unless a lot of us go out as a class. It makes things so much simpler if we keep our relationship strictly business, I mean related to your writing." The minute I used the word relationship I regretted it. From the look on his face, he seemed to take my use of that word in a way I hadn't intended.

"So you mean you'll see me after this class is over. I'd like that a lot."

Before I could answer, we both turned at the sound of someone calling my name from across the parking lot. Edna Ruth Meyers was heading toward us, a large straw hat on her head and a flowered dress enveloping her ample frame.

"Professor Martindale. Professor Martindale," she shouted. "I want to talk to you about my manuscript."

As much as I dreaded that prospect, I welcomed her arrival now. The conversation with Szabo was getting awkward.

"Forget that old bitch!" he said. "Will you see me again?"

He was persistent. I calculated how to phrase my rebuff for maximum effect.

"Look, Scott," I said, trying to hiss like a conspirator in an old World War II movie. "I know about your special relationship with Howard Phelps. I think he treated you like shit, but the whole thing shouldn't have happened in the first place. I want to make it clear that I'm not Howard Phelps. Whatever is to be between us will be strictly based on your work, nothing else."

He looked white as a sheet as I turned to face Mrs. Meyers. He slowly backed away.

"Good morning," I said cheerfully, if not sincerely. "How nice to see you on this fine spring morning."

For the next two hours, Randy and I briefed the students on their assignment before adjourning for lunch. During that entire time, Szabo kept as far away from me as possible and never once looked me in the eye.

~ ~ ~

As I walked to John Strong's office later in the day, I could hear snippets of conversation about the excitement of the night before.

". . . cut a hole in the glass . . ."

"My boyfriend said there was a lot of blood . . ."

". . . said it was probably an inside job . . ."

Little did they know. I had the advantage here—none of the technicians or secretaries I passed in the hall knew who I was or that I had had a starring role in the little drama they were talking about.

I opened the door to the director's outer office and stepped inside, trying to stifle a smile. John Strong's secretary, Grace, turned from her computer screen as I walked in.

"How are you doing, Grace?"

"Hello, Professor Martindale."

"What's all the excitement around here today?"

"Oh, someone tried to break into poor Professor Phelps's office last night."

I reacted with what I hoped was the proper mix of nonchalance and concern. I had, after all, been the one to call 911 to report a suspicious man breaking a window at the Marine Center.

"Really? What happened?"

She told me what I already knew.

"Whoever it was got away before the police got here. Did you want to see Dr. Strong?"

"Yes, I hoped to. I'm sorry, but I don't have an appointment."

"He's got a meeting in a little while, but I'll see if he's got time."

She walked through another room and into his office before returning quickly. "Dr. Strong will see you now."

Strong came out of his office and motioned me to come in. "Coffee, Tom? Cream or sugar?"

"Black, please."

He poured me a cup from a small machine sitting on a work space behind his desk.

"Am I glad this conference is over. I'm really beat. All of those high-muckety-mucks around, you media types, those demonstrators, Howard's death. Now we've got some kind of attempted break-in. Did you hear about it?"

I nodded. "Anything taken?"

"We don't think so. Whoever it was tried to climb in through a window, but ran off when the police cars drove up. A janitor working nearby didn't hear a thing."

How could she, with all that country music blaring? I thought. "Too bad."

"You've been through the mill yourself," he said. "You look like hell. I guess finding a body can do that to you."

"Yeah. Not too pleasant. And I keep smelling that carcass every time the wind blows a certain way."

"I guess the state's having trouble deciding what to do with it."
I sipped my coffee. "Dr. Strong, I'm writing an article on the whaling industry, and I'd like to get some information from you, but first I want to ask you about something else—what I hope you won't think is an impertinent question." I've never been an aggressive, in-your-face reporter. I try to slide nice and easy into subjects, especially embarrassing ones. Strong said nothing, but looked straight at me over the rim of his coffee cup. "Why did you accept the veracity of the figures in the so-called revised report and issue it so quickly as an official document?"

"What makes you say so-called? The figures were more in keeping with current scientific thinking and research. Susan Foster is a good researcher, but inexperienced. Howard Phelps is—was—an experienced scientist. His work should be vastly more . . ."

"But how can you be sure it was his work? Sue and I looked for it the day before and didn't find anything."

"You overlooked it. In all that stuff, it was easy to miss."

I was privately seething. He was calling Susan incompetent and was ready to throw her to the wolves. As far as I'm concerned, sticking up for your people is the most important part of being a good leader. But blowing up now might cost me later. John Strong could really hamper my snooping around, so I calmed down.

"Yeah. I suppose so. Sue's paying a pretty high price for her work. Do those figures become absolute gospel right away?"

"Sir Nigel took a copy with him back to London. The IWC staff will look them over, and they will be submitted to the full membership at the next meeting. That's when they go into effect."

It was time to drop this subject, much as I would have loved to argue with him about his deficiencies as a leader. "I think I have all I need for my article. I'll check with you later for anything that isn't clear. I wanted to thank you for all your help. It made it very easy to do this job. But, I was just curious about a few other things—more being nosy than anything. Did Howard Phelps have any sources of funding other than through the university?" As if I didn't know.

"He used his own private funds on occasion to pay for things," said Strong. "I didn't ask too many questions. You know there's been a real shortage of both federal and state dollars for research lately. We need all the help we can get. Howard was a bachelor—no kids, no big expenses. This job and his work meant everything to him."

"That brings me to something else. Did Howard ever make advances to his students? I mean of a sexual nature?"

"That's preposterous. If anything, he was like a male version of an old maid. Very prissy and up tight. None of the young ladies in his classes ever complained to me about that sort of thing."

"I wasn't thinking about the young ladies."

"You think Howard Phelps was queer? That's nuts. I don't even want to discuss it! The man's not even buried yet, Tom."

In spite of John Strong's growing anger, I pressed ahead. "I'm talking about Andy Kirk. Ever hear of him?"

"Of course I've heard of him. I had to sort out all the details of his disappearance. You know his body was never found. It was a tragic thing. Only child. Wealthy family. The father's some kind of hotshot surgeon in Portland. Big guy. I mean, usually you think of surgeons as being short with delicate, little hands and all that. This guy's huge, big hands and all. Why do you connect Howard with Kirk's death?"

"Kirk was one of Howard's grad students. They were on the whale expedition together. I have reason to think they were on intimate terms outside of class." I decided not to mention Scott

Szabo at this point. It seemed best to concentrate on Andy Kirk. It would be simpler that way.

"I don't believe what you're saying. Sure, Howard was there, but so were Sue Foster and three other students and the Japanese whaling scientists and a crew.

"Wait a minute. Did you say Susan Foster?"

"Yeah, so what? Howard got her on the manifest to observe Japanese whaling techniques for her research."

"She didn't mention it to me. I'm just surprised, that's all." To put it mildly. Why had Sue kept her presence on the ship a secret from me? She was obviously the other marine biologist referred to in the news story. If she was playing some kind of game with me, I didn't like it. Why was I even bothering to help her if she couldn't tell me the truth? Strong was saying something. "Sorry, what did you say?"

"I asked if you wanted to read my official report. I think it might dispel some of these crazy ideas of yours." Strong had anticipated my next request.

"Sure, I could look at it." I worked hard to keep my voice even and my face expressionless. I couldn't wait to get my hands on that report. In fact, that was the main reason I had come to see him.

He went to a small filing cabinet under the sideboard behind his desk and into his pocket for a key. "I keep all of the sensitive stuff in here. Let's see. Here it is. 'Andrew Kirk Disappearance'. You can read it and take notes if you want, but I don't want you to make any copies. It's sensitive. I probably shouldn't show this to you, but I want you to see that poor Howard had nothing to do with Kirk's disappearance. It's all in here." He patted the folder as he handed it to me. "I'll put you in my little conference room. I've got to go to a meeting. Read it and leave it on my desk when you're finished."

"I appreciate your help. I'm curious and trying to help Susan. A couple of other things before you go. What's to become of the whale carcass? And have all the delegations left Newport?"

"Some of our people are photographing and measuring the whale. Her carcass—she was an older female, you know—was pretty far gone. Smells so bad no one can stand to work downwind for very long. The highway department and state police are discussing what to do—burying her in the cove or trying to haul her to a larger land fill."

"The various delegation people?"

"Oh, sure, sorry. Let's see, the IWC man, Sir Nigel, left last night, as did the Icelandic ambassador. The Japanese delegation and the Eskimos are still in town. I think they wanted to take a few days off before heading back home."

~ ~ ~

"Andrew Kirk Disappearance" was a fairly thin document as university reports go. Strong had taken about twenty pages to recount the findings of his investigation into the loss of a university student at sea. He began by recounting the circumstances of the voyage, who was on board, and what had happened in those early morning hours almost a year before. He interviewed all the Americans and as many of the Japanese as had seemed necessary.

The university group had been allowed on board the Japanese whaling ship as observers. The ship had detoured into Oregon waters to pick them up for a voyage that would ultimately take it down the coast of the western United States and then to Central and South America. In a month's time, it would be hunting Minke whales in the Antarctic. Phelps and his students had been scheduled to stay aboard for a week.

Howard Phelps must have been a key player in whale research for the Japanese to go so far out of the way to give him a demonstration of their whaling techniques. I guess it was a payoff for his years of secret work for them and the chance to impress some wide-eyed graduate students with details of the lengths the Japanese government would go to conduct research of benefit to whale preservation. Yeah. Right. Kill them to study them. And, of course, after the research, you'd have all of that meat to dispose of to the benefit of Japanese consumers.

On the night of the second day, the entire group had eaten a large meal with the captain and most of the Japanese scientists. Lots of saké had been consumed, as well. They had all gone to bed at midnight, slightly drunk. Sometime around three in the morning, Kirk had said he was sick and left the small cabin he shared with another male student. He needed some air on deck. The bleary student murmured his understanding and went back to sleep.

At this point, the account became murky because the only witness to what had happened—Andy Kirk—was probably dead. Those on the ship and Strong in his findings assumed that young Kirk went up on deck, still dizzy from the saké, leaned over the rail to throw up, and fell overboard. His cabin mate—Scott Szabo—reported him missing when he hadn't returned in an hour.

The captain had ordered the ship to stop, then at first light to circle back along its previous route looking for any sign of life. Searchers found nothing in the choppy water. A later Coast Guard hunt also failed to locate Kirk's body.

No one had seen Kirk on deck, according to the transcripts of Strong's interviews. Only a seaman conducting a fire watch was on duty on the ship, outside of those on the bridge. They were otherwise occupied and didn't hear even a splash around the time Kirk's body is thought to have fallen over the side.

Interviews with the other students yielded nothing surprising. All had been asleep when Kirk went up on deck. Phelps had been reading in his cabin, but said he hadn't seen or heard anything unusual. The investigation reached the conclusion rather swiftly that Kirk had fallen overboard by accident.

I looked at the list of American passengers comprising Appendix A of the report. Sue's name was there as Strong said it would be. Based on that fact, a little inner voice was asking why I was knocking myself out to help her.

Szabo's name was on the list, too. It might be worth my time to talk to him about his recollections of that night. I'd need to be careful what I told him, though, because I really didn't trust him.

The report didn't say anything about Kirk's family. I did notice at the bottom of the last page among a list of those slated to get copies the name of Robert Kirk, M.D. and an address in Portland's fashionable West Hills area, the same one I had copied from the grade slips last night. Was he the DKTR K who had been driving the Mercedes that almost ran over me? Probably.

I placed the report on Strong's desk and left the building. As I walked to my car, I noticed a long black limousine parked in the area of the center's dock on Yaquina Bay across from the main building. The windows were up, but a rear door was open. I couldn't see who was sitting on the seat—only a well-tailored leg was visible—but Mr. Jima was standing there and looking at me through field glasses, an activity he made no effort to conceal, even after I had obviously spotted what he was doing.

As I drove past the road up to the dock itself, he put the glasses down and bowed slightly. What did that mean? Why was I suddenly of interest to the Japanese fisheries minister and his delegation? I watched in the rearview mirror as I made the sharp left and right turns to reach the south entrance to the Yaquina Bay Bridge; the long black car was not following me. On the way up the road to my house, I decided to stop at the Phelps's property and check on the whale carcass.

Police tape had kept the curious from crossing Phelps's property. The two deputies on duty recognized me and let me pass. I glanced at the darkened house as I walked by, wishing I could rummage around in it to look for something that might help Sue. The lingering daylight and the deputies prevented that. I noticed, however, that the house itself hadn't been sealed.

Angela Pride was standing at the top of the path above the cove, looking down.

"Good evening, sergeant. Are they making any progress?"

"Oh, hello, professor. They've decided to bury her in a huge hole. Floating the body out to sea didn't prove practical. Someone suggested blowing her up. Well, remember that case about ten years ago where somebody had the bright idea to plant dynamite under that whale that washed ashore down at Florence?"

"Yeah. I guess it was an awful mess. Smelly and damaging. I read that whale blubber flew for miles and landed on people and even ate the paint off cars."

"That has to be the worst decision ever made by whatever bureaucrat made it. So, how's your friend Ms. Foster doing?"

"Oh, I guess as well as you might expect. Jail's pretty hard to deal with when you've never been locked up before. I don't think Sheriff Kutler is cutting her any slack."

"I know he can be a hard case at times. He's an okay guy, but he does seem to have a thing about people with academic titles and degrees. He thinks they look down on him. I'm afraid they did hold Ms. Foster over for the grand jury in two days."

"I hadn't heard that. Any chance for bail?"

"Depends on what the judge says after that, but I doubt it in a murder case like this. You trying to help her? I know you used to be a magazine investigative reporter in New York and all that, but let me give you some friendly advice—stay out of the way of police investigations. You might get in the middle of something you can't get out of—I mean tampering with evidence, unauthorized entry, even obstruction of justice. I like you, Tom—may I call you that? Good. I like you, so I don't want you to get into trouble."

"Of course, I hear what you're saying, sergeant. I do get a bit too inquisitive for my own good at times. I'll be careful. I'm just curious. A reporter's curse. I need to keep my skills honed for the sake of my students."

Just then, a large bulldozer started moving the whale carcass on the beach below. The great creature seemed to heave and moan as the large steel blades touched her side. At first, it looked as though her great bulk was finally ready to submit to this large machine. But then she seemed to dig herself into the sand, not about to budge anytime soon.

9

SUNDAY, APRIL 19

THE NEXT MORNING I MADE THE DRIVE to Portland in the usual two and a half hours, first going up U.S. Highway 101, then crossing the forested slopes of the Coast Range on Oregon 18, then 22 to Salem where I picked up Interstate 5.

"State highway workers are having a whale of a time deciding what to do with the carcass of one of those huge leviathans that washed ashore near Newport several days ago with a dead scientist in its mouth. That's today's top story. News time is nine forty-five."

I kept changing stations, but most of them had the story in one form or another. I had called the telephone number listed for Dr. Kirk's residence and was told by the woman who answered that he would be home later in the morning. Even though it was Sunday, I decided to head for his house without an appointment. I gave her my name and told her to tell him that I wanted to talk to him about the disappearance of his son. I hoped that would pique his interest enough that he would see me.

Several times on the drive north, I thought I saw a blue van that seemed to be following me. I could see it several cars behind, then it would disappear. But as I drove into the outer suburbs of Portland, it was nowhere to be seen.

I turned off I-5 at the sign for the Oregon Health Sciences University and was soon on the winding boulevard that would lead me to my destination.

The Kirk home was lovely: English Tudor style, set off from the street by a large expanse of green lawn bordered on two sides by tall cedar trees. My ring was answered by a maid in full uniform—gray dress, white cap, and apron. She ushered me into a large living room off the hall. She said the doctor had gotten my message and would join me in a moment.

The top of the grand piano in the corner of the room was covered with framed photographs of the family. Over half of them were of the same person: Andy Kirk, ranging from birth to college graduation.

"What do you think of our Andy?"

The deep male voice startled me. I put down the photo I had picked up and turned to look at the tall man walking toward me with his hand extended. No question about it, he was the man who had been talking to Phelps at the center. He was an older version of the boy I had just been looking at. As John Strong had said, he was a big man.

"You're Thomas Martindale. I'm Bob Kirk. How do you do?" He motioned me to a chair on one side of the fireplace; he sat in the one opposite me. Although he was friendly, his manner was reserved and somewhat distant.

"Coffee? Carmen, please bring in the coffee things." He nodded to the maid who had reappeared so silently in the doorway that I had not seen her. "What can I do for you? Your message said something about Andy's death. Do you have some news about what happened to my son?"

"Thanks for letting me break into your Sunday, Dr. Kirk. No. I'm afraid I don't know anything more than you do. I'm working on an article on whale research at the center, and in the course of my reporting, I ran across the details of Andy's work and his unfortunate death. I thought it would make an interesting sidebar to the main article—tragic death unsolved, young career snuffed out—that sort of thing. I read the report of the university investigation and found your name on the distribution list."

I had long ago concluded in my journalistic work that while the truth can set you free, it can also at times get you in a whole lot of trouble. I could get more from Kirk, I reasoned, if I didn't mention Foster's arrest or Phelps's death—or the fact that I'd seen him before. And, I certainly wasn't going to complain that he had nearly run me down with his Mercedes.

"A whitewash. That report, I mean. The college did a slapdash job because officials were afraid I would sue. I still may do that if it would get me answers." He stopped talking as the maid set down a tray containing a coffee pot, a sugar bowl and cream pitcher, cups and saucers, linen napkins, and a plate of sweet rolls on a table between us. "Thank you, Carmen. That will be all for now. Coffee black, Mr. Martindale?"

I nodded.

"What do you think happened, Dr. Kirk?" He poured and I reached for the cup.

"My son was murdered, and I think I know who did it. That old queer Phelps. One of his professors. Took advantage of an impressionable boy. Hero worship, role model stuff. Andy wanted to be a marine scientist just like Howard Phelps, so that man's attention meant a lot to him. Going to his house for dinner, getting special help on his work. That kind of thing. His grades even went down because of all the time he spent with that predator. Then, Phelps made sexual advances to him. Andy never told me. About a month before he was lost, I found some letters in his room in Newport. I didn't tell his mother. I decided to deal with it."

"Did you confront Andy or Phelps?"

"I couldn't bring myself to ask Andy if he was gay. It was more a thing of wanting to protect him from that evil man. I went to see Phelps at his office and asked him to stop bothering Andy. He just laughed at me, said I had no evidence. He denied the letters were incriminating, said I had gotten the wrong impression from them. Said they were just signs of hero worship. I got so mad I stormed out of his office, shouting and yelling. I'm not usually like that. He was just so arrogant."

"Had you seen him recently?"

"Not for over a year."

Kirk was apparently counting on the fact that no one would remember him as one of Howard Phelps's last visitors. A whole classroom full of people had probably seen him in the doorway, but I guess he hadn't paid any attention to who might be looking at him. I had heard his shouted exchange with Phelps. But he didn't know any of that and little would be accomplished by my bringing it up now. I changed the subject.

"Do you still have the letters?"

"No. They're lost. I was afraid Andy's mother would find them. Such a discovery would have been hard on her. She has not taken our son's death very well at all. She's been institutionalized several times. She spends most of her time alone these days. I guess it's fair to say that our lives were ruined by Andy's death."

Although he was probably lying to me about the letters, I didn't feel comfortable in pressing the issue. I felt very sorry for this decent man sitting across from me. He had seen me out of kindness, and I was determined to respect his feelings. Also, the fact remained that I wasn't a policeman and he wasn't under suspicion. That was fairly well understood by both of us. I couldn't do anything to him. But he hadn't needed to see me and he had been willing to do so. I finished my second cup of coffee and sweet roll and got up to leave.

"Dr. Kirk, I want to thank you for seeing me. I know it is difficult to bring up these unpleasant memories."

He looked surprised that I was leaving so quickly.

"That's okay. But we haven't talked about Andy's work. He was awfully proud of his research. Nothing earthshaking, you understand, but not bad for a grad student. I guess that's a father bragging." His voice trailed off and he turned his face away.

"Dr. Kirk, I haven't been honest with you. A close friend has been arrested for Howard Phelps's murder. I'm trying to help clear her name, and I thought there might be a connection to Andy's disappearance."

"I heard about Phelps on the news. I can't say I'm sorry." His sad eyes suddenly hardened as he thought of his old enemy. He didn't seem angry about my deception. "I'm sorry about your friend. I don't think I've been of much help."

He walked me to the front door. I wanted to ask him where he had been on the night of Howard Phelps's death, but just couldn't bring myself to do it. "Thanks again. It was good to meet you. I hope your wife gets to feeling better soon."

"I'm afraid there isn't much chance of that."

As I walked to my car, I caught a glimpse of the blue van turning the corner of the next block. Who was that guy? My heart rate elevated a bit as I unlocked my car door and sat down, relocking the door behind me. I checked the lock on the passenger side, too—just in case. I turned the car around and headed downtown in the opposite direction.

My destination was Powell's, the largest bookstore in the state. My isolation on the coast had prevented me from finding several books I had read reviews about. No matter how modest my salary, I could always scrape together enough money for books. Besides, I loved to browse through the endless shelves in a real bookworm's heaven.

I drove my car up the narrow, steep incline of the parking garage adjacent to the bookstore. I'd always thought the ancient structure must have been designed for Model Ts, with ramps and turning radii that were much too narrow for today's automobiles. I feared I would scrape the sides of my car as I drove along. I found a spot on the second level and walked back to the street to step around the corner to the store itself. Even though it was midday, the structure was dimly lighted.

I spent more than two hours roaming the aisles. Powell's is such a large bookstore that clerks give you a map of the color-coded sections as you walk in the door. That always suits me just fine because the hunt for the books I want is part of the fun. This is much better than stores where officious employees constantly follow you around asking if they can help you.

As I rounded the journalism section, I almost knocked someone down. "Sorry, I wasn't look—"

"Hi, Professor Martindale. Fancy meeting you here. You look great. Love your suit and that tie."

Scott Szabo was dressed in tighter clothes than he wore in Newport. He even had an earring in his left ear, something I don't think he sported at the coast. As we spoke, he put his arm around the nice-looking Latino man who was with him and pulled him close.

"This is my Portland friend, Carlo."

The young man gave me a quick look from top to bottom, sizing me up before he put out his hand, which I shook.

"How's it going?" I asked politely.

"Is he the one you had the hots for, Scotty? I mean last week's candidate?" Saying that, Carlo put his head back and laughed loudly and a little too long. Szabo smiled and pretended to put a hand over the other man's mouth as a way to shut him up. But he didn't seem a bit embarrassed at what his friend had said. I ignored the comment.

"Scott, I'm glad to run into you. I've been meaning to ask you about the night Andy Kirk was lost at sea. I hear you were on the trip."

"Yeah, but I didn't see anything. I slept through it all. I guess I drank too much, and it really knocked me out. But I might remember something if you stop by Carlo's apartment for a drink." He wrote a telephone number on a white card and handed it to me. "Here's where I'll be. We could talk about it some more."

"I . . . uh . . . don't think that would be such a good idea, Scott. I need to get back to the coast tonight. I'll ask you about that night another time."

"I could put you up, professor," added Carlo, who winked at Scott.

"Maybe some other time," I replied, adding under my breath, "in another lifetime." I said goodbye and paid for my books.

Back up on the second level, I felt uneasy as I approached my car. The low ceiling made me suddenly claustrophobic and short of breath. I picked up the pace considerably, my shoes making loud tapping noises on the cement floor. Only my dignity prevented me from breaking into an all out run to my car.

Just then, a man with long hair stepped in front of me from behind a thick pillar. I jumped.

"What do you want?"

The shadow created by his wide-brimmed black hat hid his face. "You've got information we need to know, Martindale," his voice said gruffly.

"I don't know what . . ."

Then the dark world of Powell's parking structure got even darker. I hoped I wouldn't fracture my skull as I fell to the cement.

10

IT WAS STILL LIGHT when I regained consciousness. I had a terrible headache. From the location of the big knot on my head, I knew I had been struck from behind—a real conk, but no blood. A real neat hit. I squinted at my watch. I'd been out about a half-hour. Oddly, I was seated in my car, behind the wheel—seeming to be taking a nap, if anyone noticed me. I took a quick survey; my wallet was intact, my books on the seat beside me.

This must been the work of the guys in the blue van. But what were they looking for? What did they think I knew? And who were they?

I had to get out of here, but I certainly didn't feel like driving back to the coast. I was afraid that I might black out on the freeway or get sick on the winding road through the Coast Range.

So, what should I do? I didn't particularly want to go to a hotel. I remembered something about not going to sleep if you have a concussion, which I probably had. The police weren't an option either—all those questions with answers I didn't want to give.

I didn't visit Portland all that often, so I didn't know very many people—a few former students, some acquaintances among journalists I'd covered some stories with. I certainly didn't want to call Scott Szabo at Carlo's apartment and go over there.

Dr. Kirk. Even in my groggy state, Andy Kirk's father seemed the most logical person to consult. Although I barely knew him, he might help me. Besides, he was a doctor.

I started the car and turned on the lights, hoping I could navigate through the narrow confines of the garage. I steered the car carefully down the ramp, hitting one or two rubber cones as I did. As I neared the main entrance, I slowed down to hand the attendant my validated ticket which, miraculously, I had located sticking out of one of my new books. That done, I picked up speed a bit too much in my descent to the street. My car hit bottom as I entered the roadway, causing me to hit my head on the ceiling on the rebound. I had forgotten to put on my seat belt.

I pulled over to the side to rest for a minute and make sure I wasn't too dizzy to drive. My head felt like an iron anvil was sitting on top of it, but the world wasn't spinning. A good sign? I didn't have a clue.

Driving slow enough to be safe but not so slow as to become a traffic hindrance, I made my way back to the Kirk house in the West Hills. It was nearly six when I parked in front of the doctor's residence. I walked unsteadily up the walk and rang the doorbell. This time, Kirk himself opened the door.

"Martindale, what the hell? . . ."

His words sounded faintly in my ears, as I blacked out and collapsed on his doorstep.

~ ~ ~

"Here, drink this slowly. It's whiskey." He put his arm under my head to get it high enough so I wouldn't choke. It was so strong, I did anyway. "Take it easy. Keep coughing to clear your windpipe. God, I feel a nasty knot on your head. Let's see." He pressed the bump gently with both thumbs. Although it really hurt, I didn't cry out. "Lie back gently. It's a big bump, but the skin isn't broken and there's no blood. You passed out from the trauma to your system. A mild kind of shock. What happened?"

After another sip of whiskey, I told Kirk everything that had taken place. He seemed interested, no doubt because of my vague involvement with what happened to Andy. He sat in a high-backed wing chair and sipped wine while he listened.

"And you have no idea who these guys were?"

"No idea. It's got to be someone interested in what I've found out."

"And you really haven't found anything out . . . or have you?" For a moment, Kirk seemed agitated when he asked the question, which struck me as odd.

"I keep hitting dead ends. I think it's time to get back to what I like to think I do best—writing and teaching writing. I'm out of my league here. And I've got to think of my head. It won't last very long if people keep hitting it."

I reached up to touch the bump and winced from the pain even this slight contact created.

"Better not touch it. The swelling will go down overnight, and you'll be able to drive back to the coast in the morning. Guaranteed." He was smiling, the agitation of a few moments ago completely gone. "Do you feel like eating? Carmen has fixed her specialty, a chicken dish that will melt in your mouth. Why don't you wash your face and join me in the dining room? The bathroom's back there."

I sat up carefully and swung my legs over the edge of the sofa. Either I was feeling better or the whiskey had dulled all the pain.

"Here's a clean shirt. If it's too large, you can roll up the sleeves."

Because my own was wrinkled and torn, Kirk threw a blue dress shirt at me that he got out of a closet in the corner of the room. I jumped to my feet to catch it and, for once, the room didn't whirl around me. I was feeling better.

~ ~ ~

Dinner lived up to his advance billing. The chicken, vegetables, and what tasted like homemade rolls were all excellent. I decided to forgo the wine since my head was hazy enough already.

Kirk's own imbibing had loosened his tongue considerably. "I'm sorry my wife couldn't join us, Tom. As I mentioned this morning, she hasn't been herself since Andy disappeared. She really doted on him. She couldn't have any more children, so he was all . . ." He turned his head and bit his lip. I hardly knew what to say.

"I can't imagine the empty feeling after something like this. You have your work, I guess. Your wife has . . ."

". . . her memories. She won't move on. She doesn't have any hobbies or favorite charities. She spends her days looking at scrapbooks and hugging old Teddy bears. Which reminds me, I'd better look in on her. And, I'm suddenly feeling rather tired myself."

He stood up so quickly that his chair tipped over backwards. The loud clatter brought Carmen rushing through the door to the kitchen.

"I'm fine. I just got up too fast. Carmen, the professor will be our guest tonight. Tom, I've enjoyed our time together. I have an early surgery in the morning, so sleep as late as you wish. Carmen will give you breakfast and see you off for me."

"I can't thank you enough. You really saved my life—or at least my head."

We both laughed as we shook hands. Then he turned and walked rather unsteadily through the door, tears running down his face. Carmen, a plump woman with beautiful black hair, only shook her head in sadness.

~ ~ ~

Something woke me in the middle of the night. The clock on the nightstand read three forty-five. I sat up carefully to test my head and listened. Sleep really is a great healer—I felt a lot better. I got up and walked to the window. Last night, Carmen had directed me to a guest room upstairs in what appeared to be another wing of the house. Now, as I looked out, I realized that I could see right into the windows of rooms in the main part of the house.

After my eyes had adjusted to the darkness, I spotted the source of the noise that had awakened me. A blonde woman was on her knees in front of another figure whose face was obscured by a lamp. She seemed to be sobbing.

I turned away because I felt like such an intruder. This had to be Mrs. Kirk and the doctor had to be trying to comfort her. Suddenly, their words came wafting across the open space.

". . . stifling in here, Adelle . . . middle of the night . . . back to bed."

"Robert . . . boy is gone . . . him back to me . . . can't live without him."

". . . about me? . . . your husband."

As I pulled the drapes, Dr. Kirk had fallen to his knees and was holding his wife.

11

MONDAY, APRIL 20

State highway workers are having a whale . . ."

COULDN'T THESE NEWS READERS change the construction of the story at least a bit? I kept punching buttons on the car radio to blot out the story on my drive home the next morning, but to no avail. The subject was just too bizarre for the news stations to resist. The call-in shows were worse.

"They need to fill that whale with hot-air balloons, and then she'll float out to sea on her own."

"Thank you, Fred from Philomath."

"I'd get me an Uzi and fill that baby with so many holes there'd be nothin' left to smell bad."

"Thank you, Lester from Tillamook."

"This whole thing is part of the conspiracy by the CIA and the Japanese fishing industry to kill every whale for the meat. It's all in the records stored in those salt caverns in New Mexico."

"Thank you, Moonflower from Eugene."

I turned the radio off, happier to be alone with my thoughts. I hadn't been able to sleep after seeing the Kirks so I got up, showered, and dressed. I left Kirk a note of appreciation and slipped out a side door. After getting some breakfast in an all-night diner in Wilsonville, I had driven home in just over two hours and pulled into the driveway of my house in Newport shortly after seven.

Before going inside, I walked over to Phelps's property to check on the progress of the men working on the whale carcass. From my vantage point on the cliff, I could see that they hadn't done very much. The stench from rotting skin and blubber was even stronger than before, so I didn't hang around.

Happily, I didn't have any lingering effects from the blow on my head and felt fine as I unpacked the car. Once that was done, I made a pot of coffee and sat down to take stock of things and figure out what I knew up to this point. Howard Phelps was dead, probably killed because he played fast and loose with people's lives and data that he may have been selling to the highest bidder. Susan Foster had been arrested for his murder. Although I couldn't prove it, I didn't think she had done it. Even though I was still angry with her for not telling me everything, I knew I would continue to help her.

With so much on my mind, I knew it was futile to try to concentrate on writing, so I decided to press on with my investigation. I reached for the telephone.

"Newport Hilton? Do you have someone named Nagamo staying there? Yes, with the whale conference. Ring his room for me, please? Thank you.

"Is this the room of Mr. Nagamo? My name is Thomas Martindale. I'm a writer covering the conference. I was calling to see if I could ask the minister some questions for my article. A lot of it is background."

Whoever I had gotten on the line was checking with someone in the background.

There was no mistaking the loud grunt that preceded the next voice I heard. "Hello," said Mr. Jima.

"Tom Martindale here. We met the other day when you came to get Susan Foster. I was with her when you . . ."

"I remember you, professor."

"Good. Did your assistant tell you what I want?"

"An interview with His Excellency."

"Yes. Just a few questions for an article I'm writing."

"His Excellency has instructed me to invite you to be his guest for lunch today at noon in the dining room of our hotel."

Before I could answer, he hung up.

~ ~ ~

The ambassador was sitting alone at the table by a window when I walked in. Mr. Jima was seated at the next table with another man, presumably the one who had answered the phone. He was small and shy looking, perhaps the ambassador's male secretary, not another bodyguard. Mr. Jima handled that without any help, I was certain. He stood up and motioned for me to approach. As I did so, he looked me over, but did not pat me down as I thought he might. The ambassador rose and bowed to me as we shook hands, and then we both sat down.

"Professor Martindale. A pleasure. I've read some of your articles. You are very knowledgeable about whales for a non-scientist. The fisheries industry could use help such as yours in getting its story out to American readers."

Was he trying to buy me off to nullify whatever he thought I had found out about him? Or was he just being polite?

"Thank you, Mr. Nagamo. I am honored that you like my work." I was sounding slightly Japanese myself, having lapsed into formal, stilted phrases one would hear at the court of a king—or in this case, I guess, an emperor. "I wanted to ask you why the Japanese government continued to demand the right to kill whales even in the face of so much opposition from all over the world."

He straightened up in his chair and seemed prepared to give me a formal discourse on the subject, when a waiter appeared.

"Good afternoon. My name is Todd. I'll be your server today. Something from the bar?"

"A Johnny Walker on the rocks." Minister Nagamo didn't hesitate, then nodded to me.

"Iced tea, please."

"Plain or mint?"

"Plain, I guess."

"Can I tell you about our specials for luncheon today?"

"I have decided to have the crab cakes. Professor Martindale?"

"The club sandwich on wheat bread."

Todd wrote down our orders, looking disappointed by our refusal to let him recite the list of daily specials. He nodded his head and moved to Jima's table behind us. "Good afternoon. My name is Todd. I'll be your server today. Something from the bar?"

I tuned out, but was mildly curious about what the huge man would eat. I decided I could always peek when his meal was served.

"I was about to explain my government's position, I believe." Nagamo was not missing a beat.

"People in my country have eaten whale meat for centuries. We couldn't get it in sufficient quantities during the war, but your General MacArthur saw to it that our ships were outfitted and allowed to set sail in 1946. The fleet has continued to expand and sail greater distances to get the whales we need to feed our people."

"But why do you still do this in view of worldwide denunciation? Can't other kinds of meat be substituted?"

"How would Americans like to be told that they would have to find a substitute for meat and poultry? How would you feel as a people if an outside organization ordered you to quit killing cows and chickens, Professor Martindale?"

"Cows and chickens are not endangered and protected species, Mr. Minister. Cows and chickens are dumb creatures without the intelligence of whales."

"Professor Martindale, I fear you have bought into conservationist propaganda. Don't let their size or the fact that they breathe air lead you to think that whales have souls. They are just dumb animals like all others."

"I don't want to argue with you. Why don't we agree to disagree on that point?"

" 'Agree to disagree.' A nice American saying. That fits well in this situation, I believe. Very well. We will, as you say, move on. It is my government's position that while whales in danger of extinction can be protected, whales in great abundance can be killed for commercial purposes. I can assure you that the exploding harpoons we use today cause instant death. There is no suffering. We try to use all the meat. We do not kill whales as trophies, Mr. Martindale. It is not like a big-game hunt for us. There are no whales stuffed and mounted on the walls of game rooms."

"I don't deny that fact. I deplore it, but I can't deny it. To move on to another subject, I wondered how significant Professor Foster's population numbers are to you."

There was a lull in the conversation as the waiter served our lunches. Interviewing someone over a meal can create certain problems. You have to carry on the interview (trying not to ask questions when your mouth is full) and take notes as you handle a fork at the same time.

"We wanted to hear what they were so as to determine whether we could conduct our fall hunt in Antarctica."

"You hoped for high numbers, then? Higher than you got from Professor Foster's report?"

"One doesn't hope for such things in my business. One listens and deals with what one hears. And, of course, in this case those figures were corrected later. The new ones are very favorable to us. Our ships can sail after all. We wished for better figures, and our dreams came true. The wish was, how do you say it, father to the thought."

Minister Nagamo was combining Asian inscrutability with Western sayings my grandmother would appreciate. We both continued eating our lunches. I decided against accusing him and his government of having something to do with falsifying the data. I glanced around the room and noticed that Damon Istook from the Alaska Eskimo Whaling Commission had walked in and was being seated several tables away. Although we had never been formally introduced, we knew who each other was. He nodded at me as he sat down, no doubt wondering what the Japanese fisheries minister would have to say to me.

"Does the Japanese government prop up the whaling industry? I mean by paying for its ships and buying whale meat to keep prices high?"

"My government has a long history of supporting crucial elements of its industry."

"But why whaling? Surveys I've seen show that Japanese young people have no interest in eating whale meat."

The minister's face reddened at my effrontery. "Your facts are just plain wrong, Mr. Martindale. My people consider whale meat a delicacy and an important part of their culture."

We were nearly finished. As Todd, the officious server, prepared to clear the dishes and, no doubt, hustle the dessert tray out from the back, I decided it was time to ask my only really controversial question.

"What is the Hirakawa Research Foundation, Mr. Minister?"

Once again, Nagamo's inscrutability slipped a bit. I could see surprise flash across his eyes for a brief moment. "I was not aware that the Hirakawa Research Foundation was known in your country. It is a private Japanese scientific institution that supports research on marine life and the ocean in general. I know very little else about it."

"I hate to contradict you, but I've seen their letterhead, and I also noted your name on a list of the board of directors."

Nagamo's irritation with me was growing. He raised his hand and snapped his fingers. In an instant, Mr. Jima was on his feet, almost tipping over his strawberry shortcake in the process. Minister Nagamo rose and bowed toward me.

"Our conversation is finished. Your lunch will be paid for. It has been a pleasure getting to know you on a more personal basis."

I stood up, too. I wasn't finished with my questioning. Why not make a person even more angry once you've got him only partly steamed?

"Did Hirakawa fund the research projects of Professor Howard Phelps?" That I asked the question at all implied that I already knew the answer.

"I think our interview will be over now," Nagamo replied, then he leaned toward me before departing. "I would advise you to confine your reporting to things of a less controversial nature, Professor Martindale."

He was whispering, but his anger was unmistakable. Mr. Jima glowered, too, as if to emphasize his boss's growing contempt for me. The entire entourage left the room. I sat down and sorted through my notes as I finished my iced tea.

12

TUESDAY, APRIL 21

I WOKE UP THE NEXT MORNING feeling stiff and sore, like I'd had the flu for a month, with the aftereffects of a wild party thrown in. I didn't answer the phone until it had rung several times.

"Hello."

"Professor Martindale? This is Damon Istook of the Alaska Eskimo Whaling Commission."

"Oh, yes, sir. I've seen you around the IWC meeting. In fact, I was planning to call you. I'm writing an article on whales and whaling. I found the discussion about Bowheads and Eskimo culture very interesting."

"I think you need an Eskimo point of view," he replied. "I couldn't help seeing you having lunch with Minister Nagamo yesterday. Could we meet today? I know where you live. I could come to your house."

I didn't really like the fact that so many people knew so much about me and where I was living. My place was fairly isolated. Besides, it hadn't been very long since I was hit on the head.

"I'd rather meet you at the Marine Center library. I can get us the conference room; we won't be bothered there. Shall we say in one hour—at ten A.M.? See you then."

In the shower and while I was shaving, I thought about how whatever I would get from Damon Istook would fit into my article. Eskimo whaling was controversial. I gathered the Eskimos were not happy about Susan's population numbers; as with everyone else, they would benefit from a bigger quota because that would allow them to kill more whales. But whether they had anything to do with Howard Phelps's murder was another question entirely.

~   ~   ~

Several Eskimos with long hair, big black hats, and dark glasses were standing around a stretch limousine parked near the public wing of the Marine Center when I drove up. Newport had probably never before seen this many long, sleek cars. I couldn't see through the tinted glass to know if anyone was seated in the back. I didn't relish even a brief encounter with all the muscle standing around the car, so I made my way up the walk and through the public wing, again entering the Staff Only door as if I owned the place. Everyone was casual here and didn't get too up tight about trespassers. The library was small and hard to find, up some stairs in a back corridor.

Damon Istook was already there, alone and reading what looked like a fisheries journal, as I walked up and officially introduced myself. "Tom Martindale. We're both early."

"My pleasure, Tom. Please call me Damon. Can we have some privacy?"

"Yes, back through here."

I had called ahead to arrange for the use of the conference room. We entered and sat down facing each other in the middle of a long table.

"I am very interested in Eskimo culture as it relates to whaling," I began.

Istook had anticipated my question and pulled out a slick-looking four-color brochure on just that subject. "You look surprised that we would have something this professional."

I shook my head and started to speak. He raised his hand and cut me off.

"Ever since the Alaska Eskimo Whaling Commission was formed in 1977 to convince the U.S. government to take action to preserve our Bowhead hunt, we knew we would have to compete in the same way our adversaries do. We hired an Anchorage public relations firm and a lobbyist in D.C. You still look surprised."

"Well, no. I just . . . "

"You expected Nanook of the North? We aren't toothless savages who eat seal blubber all day long and screw our women all night in our igloos."

"I just think it is fascinating that you use your resources so well. I hadn't realized you needed a lobbyist in Washington."

"If we didn't, we'd get screwed even more than we do already. Let me explain our situation."

"Mind if I take notes? I want to get all of this right."

"No, that's fine. Now, hunting Bowhead whales has been part of our culture for centuries. Every season our hunters sail out from small villages along the Alaskan coast in the Bering Sea to get whales. You see, the Bowheads migrate beginning in late March from Soviet waters in the Chukchi Sea . . ."—he was pointing to a map on one of the panels of the brochures—". . . through the Bering Strait and on up around the top of Alaska into the Beaufort Sea. They go east into Canadian waters, where they spend the summer. They follow the ice pack as it recedes, so it's quite slow going for them.

"As the whales make their journey, our hunters go out from their small villages in umiaks—seal skin boats—and kill whales with their harpoons. They've done this for years. It is a rite of passage for our young men. Many of our older hunters believe that the whales sacrifice themselves for the good of the village. A whaling village participates in the hunt, both at sea and on shore, and we hold special ceremonies associated with it. You know, a whole village can live a year on the meat of *one* whale—they're sometimes fifty feet long and weigh seventy-five to one hundred metric tons. We also use the skin and the baleen . . . Do you know what that is?"

I nodded, thinking instantly of the hole cut in the baleen of the Gray whale I had found, the hole cut so Phelps's body could be slipped inside.

"The baleen is what did in the Bowheads during the last century. The so-called Yankee whalers from New Bedford, Massachusetts, and other ports first sailed into the Arctic in the eighteen fifties. During the next sixty years, they killed thousands of Bowheads, primarily for their baleen and to a lesser extent their oil. The baleen was needed to make buggy whips and chair seat springs and even corset stays. It was a terrible waste of whales—wholesale slaughter really. Nobody regulated it and nobody cared, except my people, who had no power to do anything. The stupid ones worked for the white men in charge of the slaughter. The wise ones knew that our culture was threatened with so many whales being killed—for nothing but greed. It all ended when spring steel and petroleum replaced the raw material the whales were yielding."

Istook's face was sober. What he was saying was tragic, a sad preview of what would happen to the Eskimos themselves—exploited and abandoned.

"So, what happened after the white hunters left?" I asked him.

"Our people gradually got back to the subsistence hunting we had done historically. We still need the Bowhead to keep our villages together. It's a tremendous force for unity in the village."

"But it's so difficult to work in that environment. I mean all the cold and ice. I'm surprised your people are so keen to continue doing this."

"What choice do they have? It's in their souls!"

"Could you give me some idea of the conditions up there?"

"I'll tell you this: it's so cold in these polar regions that sea water freezes. This can create ice that is nine feet thick. Ice first appears in the Bering Strait in September or October. It spreads gradually southward until, in deep winter, nearly two-thirds of the surface of the Bering Sea is covered with ice. In the Chukchi and Beaufort Seas, the polar pack never melts. Only the southern portions of those seas become temporarily free of ice in summer. By June, the air temperatures finally rise above freezing, but then the cold is replaced with fog."

I asked him about his people's reaction when the International Whaling Commission set strict quotas for the number of whales they could hunt.

"Everyone was pretty pissed," he said. "The IWC doesn't understand how much the Bowheads mean to us. Also, their count is way too low. What it seemed to us was that some bureaucrat in London or Washington or some place like that was telling us what we could do, how many whales they would let us kill. Pardon me, Mr. Martindale, but that's just bullshit!"

"You don't think any of it is aimed at saving a species so it won't be completely killed off? You know, things do become extinct."

"Okay, okay. I agree with you—to a point. It's just that we don't think those first census figures were any good. Way too low. The revisions were a lot better. More realistic. Some years we only get to kill a few Bowheads. I mean, we've got fifteen or twenty villages that want to hunt. And they give us five as a quota! Ridiculous! It wouldn't have worked!"

"You came here hoping for more whales in the total count, I guess. So your quota would be higher?"

"Yeah. We do our own informal counting. And our numbers were higher. The IWC won't use our numbers. Said they're biased. So then we're stuck. They won't budge. And I've got to make our people accept what they give us, but it's not always that easy. The new numbers will help."

"What can I do?"

"I just want you to write a fair story, a story that asks the IWC to keep our quota up."

"I want to help, but you don't understand the kind of article I'm writing. I can't really express my opinion; that's done in editorials. What I can do is present the facts in such a way that my readers will demand action. That's how it's done. It can't be heavy-handed. It's got to be as sophisticated as I can make it."

"Yeah. I guess I see." He got up and shook my hand. "Let me know if you need anything else from me."

"One more question. Do you have any connection to the Japanese?"

"Those bastards. They set us back with their constant demands and bogus research. Besides, they don't want the same kind of whales we want. No, there's no connection. They do their thing before the IWC, we do ours. I really get mad, though, when they try to claim that their whaling is subsistence whaling too—like ours. That's really stretching things quite a lot. Well, see you around. Thanks for listening."

He turned on his heel and was gone.

~ ~ ~

As I drove home that night, I got to thinking about my involvement in all of this. What business did I have looking into a murder? There was my desire to help Susan Foster, a good friend. Then there was my nosiness. Every reporter has to have that quality, and I hadn't lost it just because I had entered the academic world. In this case, I was simply trying to figure out who had killed Howard Phelps and why. It was odd that so much of what I was finding out dealt with whales and, at least indirectly, could work into my articles.

I stopped these musings abruptly as I drove past Phelps's house. I could see what looked like flashlights shining at the back, near the cliff above the cove. I parked my car in my driveway, then edged along the path from my yard, across another one, to his. It was a back way that would allow me to observe his house and rear yard without being seen. Although the cove ran behind all three houses, it could only be entered from his yard.

Apparently, no one had used this back path for some time, evidenced by how overgrown those damn blackberry vines were. I decided to ease along and take a peek. Nothing to be seen—no light, no person. The door was closed, and the house looked untouched.

At this hour, no one from the whale removal crew was around. The guy from the stranding network had apparently taken his samples to be analyzed and was waiting for results. I guess the job was not high enough on any highway department priority list to merit overtime. Those guys didn't have to put up with the putrid smell, which wafted toward my house whenever the wind was right—or wrong.

As I stood on the edge shining my flashlight onto the beach, I was suddenly hit by a body block that sent me tumbling over the edge. My surprise was quickly replaced by fear as I began to career downward along the narrow and crumbling path.

Would I be joining the whale on the sand? My heart was pounding as I desperately tried to stop myself from falling into the cove.

13

I WAS ABLE TO GRAB HOLD of a slightly exposed tree root along the path. That broke my fall. I lay on my side, panting and coughing, for a few minutes before getting up on my knees in preparation to stand and face whoever or whatever had hit me.

"Are you all right?" A soft voice was coming from the top. "Trog didn't mean to hurt you. He just gets a little carried away sometimes. He was trying to protect me."

I kept quiet, but got my flashlight ready. Miraculously, I had held onto it during my tumble. It felt practically welded to my hand.

"Give him your hand. He'll help you up."

I turned on my light and immediately saw two faces peering down at me. The woman was Mara from the seminar. The man was her giant bodyguard. Would he pull me up just so he could work me over some more or could I trust him? The guy deserved a shove himself, but he was a hell of a lot bigger than I, and I was feeling a bit off-balance. I wasn't in much of a position to delay very long, though, so I decided to take a chance and grab his outstretched hands. He yanked, and I was quickly back up on top. I stood up and brushed myself off, wondering if this cove would eventually ruin all of my clothes.

"What are you doing here?"

"We might ask the same of you."

"I live here—or at least two doors down. I was looking after this house and checking to see if that dead whale was gone. One beached here last week . . ."

". . . and a dead man wound up in the mouth," Mara interrupted. "A great way for a conservationist to die, but Howard Phelps was no conservationist. He was in league with the Japanese!"

My interest was piqued, but I still didn't completely trust this pair. Her vague kindness seemed a bit forced, and he was unpredictable. How could I find out what she knew without putting myself in danger?

"Professor. Professor!"

The three of us turned toward the sound of the shouts, which were coming from the side of the house. Once again, Edna Ruth Meyers had inadvertently presented me a solution to a problem, not to mention rescuing me from a rather tight spot.

"Oh, there you are. And Mara and Mr. Trog. How nice. Are you holding some kind of field exercise?"

"Er . . . a . . . something like that. Hello, Mrs. Meyers." I moved quickly to her side, grabbing her elbow to steer her into our little conclave. I was already regretting how quickly I had brushed off her requests for me to read her manuscript.

"Thank you, professor," she said, her body rocking from side to side. "The ground is rather uneven here."

"It's good to see you again," I said, bowing slightly. "What brings you out here?" I was plunging ahead with my own agenda, ignoring Mara and Trog for the time being and banking on my feeling that he wouldn't hurt two of us.

"I got your address from the director's secretary. I hope it's all right. I wanted to bring my article to let you read my first draft—you know, to help me improve any rough spots."

"I'd be delighted," I said. "Why don't we all go over to my house where we can be more comfortable?" I looked at Mara in time to see her give Trog a slight nod.

Mrs. Meyers took the younger woman's arm in hers and began to propel her toward the road. "How grand," she said. "Come on, Mara, let's go get some tips on writing from a real pro. And Mr. Trog, you come along too."

The large man meekly followed our little entourage as we walked around Phelps's house. Mrs. Meyers had brought about a remarkable transformation in both Mara and Trog.

Mara started talking as we walked down the street to my house. "We looked you up in the files of our organization," she said. "You're famous—at least you're in our files!"

"Why doesn't that please me?" I said. "What files do you mean?"

"Sorry. I really haven't told you much about us. We are representatives in Oregon for Earth and Sea, a worldwide environmental group. We are trying to save the whales and the redwoods and stop pollution and get the air cleaned up—and lots of other things. Our organization has compiled a lot of material on all kinds of subjects and people."

I led them down the road, the proper way to go. I was sick of all this skulking around in the bushes. I hoped that my quick value judgment of Mara's harmlessness and ability to control Trog were valid. I hoped my quick assessment of the two of them would not prove fatal to Mrs. Meyers and me.

It only took a few minutes for our rather strange little group to walk down the road to my house. As I unlocked the door, she whispered something in the giant's ear. He listened intently and nodded. As we walked in the door, he sat down outside, folding his arms across his chest.

"Come in. Do you want coffee?" I said to them all, then to Mara, "Isn't your friend coming in?"

"No. I told him to wait outside. It's all right. He's used to it."

I turned on lights in the living room, took off my coat, and laid it over a chair. Then I went to the kitchen and started making the coffee. The women followed me in and sat down at the wooden table by the back window.

"Nice place. You lived here long?" asked Mrs. Meyers.

"I'm renting it while I'm on leave; I've been here less than a month."

I turned to Mara who was looking out the window.

"Now, you want to tell me what this is all about? Why were you at Phelps's house, and why did your friend attack me?"

"That part is easy. He acts as kind of an unofficial bodyguard for me."

"You couldn't prove it by me—the unofficial part, I mean. Why do you need a bodyguard?" As I moved around in the kitchen, my side started bothering me. I was sure it was bruised.

"He gets a little worked up at times. What we do can be a bit dangerous. He knows I won't stop once I've decided what I want to do. So he stands by to bail me out."

"Oh dear," said Mrs. Meyers.

"How dangerous does it get?" I asked. "What do you do? Are you guys like Greenpeace? I mean, chaining yourselves to things or sailing in front of battleships?"

"Or whaling ships," said Mara. "Yes, we've done stuff like that. Earth and Sea is a worldwide organization dedicated to saving whales and redwoods and . . ."

"I know," I said. "You already told me. But that's brochure copy. What do you really do, and what's in Howard Phelps's house that's so important to you?"

"You're right," Mara answered. "No more rhetoric. I promise. You seem like a good person, Professor Martindale, so I'll be candid with you. We have reason to believe that Howard Phelps betrayed us to the Japanese."

"Oh my," gasped Mrs. Meyers. "How awful!"

"We think he revealed the name of one of our officers who had gone undercover and infiltrated the crew of a Korean pirate whaling operation," Mara said. "We were going to look for evidence in his house, but we couldn't get in."

"Pirate whaling?" I asked. "You mean like men with eye patches and wooden legs who carry parrots on their shoulders?"

"Not movie pirates. I mean outlaw crews who hunt whales wherever and whenever they please. They ignore IWC quotas— do you know what that means?"

I nodded and reached for a yellow legal pad and a pencil.

"May I take notes on this?"

"I guess so . . . sure, why not?" Mara said. "Anyway, we feel they ignore the quotas and kill any whale they encounter on voyages in the Pacific, from off Asia down to the Antarctic. Then they sell the whale meat to Japan. Although it's not supposed to, the Japanese government buys the whale meat. Some people even suspect that the Japanese government bankrolls the pirate operations."

"Oh dear!" said Mrs. Meyers.

"Can you prove it?" I asked. "That's a very serious charge."

"We'd love to, but it's difficult. We keep trying, though."

"Aren't you fighting a futile battle? I mean the odds of prevailing against any well-financed government operation are great. It seems like everything is stacked against you."

Mara sighed and went on. "We have to keep trying for small victories here and there. The smaller groups like Earth and Sea have most of the political power in this fight. When we have to, we can concentrate on one issue and stick with it. The really large environmental/conservation groups don't like to get into big conflicts, like consumer boycotts and heavy-duty legislation. They are too bureaucratic and slow moving. Good God, the big ones wouldn't even endorse the Save the Whales campaign when it first started. They just don't want to make a big benefactor mad. We tend more toward acts of civil disobedience. Like Greenpeace, we frequently go further than most other groups are comfortable with."

She paused to drink some coffee, which gave me time to catch up in my note taking.

"So, about this pirate whaling—what more can you tell me?"

She ran her fingers through her hair as she contemplated an answer. She really had all of this stuff memorized.

"We're trying to end it. Pirate whaling ships are like seventeenth-century counterparts. They sail the seas and do what they want and nobody stops them. Their crews ignore IWC regulations and slaughter whales when they find them. We do our best to stop them, but a lot of governments look the other way and let them operate out of their ports. And it all means that hundreds of whales will be killed for nothing but greed."

"Oh my!" said Mrs. Meyers.

Our coffee cups were empty, and Mara looked drained. Her voice was cracking; tears ran down her cheeks. Edna Ruth got up and walked over to comfort the younger woman.

"There, there, dear. Don't cry. Professor Martindale will help you."

"Thank you for telling me all of this," I said. "It really helps me to understand what your group has been doing—and what you're up against. I'm not sure how much I can do except put all of this in an article I'm writing. Does that seem all right with you?"

She looked up and dried her eyes with her sleeve. "Sure. Publicity keeps us going. But I'm probably not a good person to quote. I'm . . . just a peon. You need a name . . . one of our officers, perhaps."

"Whatever you think. I'd also like some documentation. It's not that I don't trust . . ."

"I know. I can get that for you and get someone to call you from our headquarters. And this might be something you'd find useful." Mara reached into her bag and handed me a publication with the Earth and Sea logo on the cover. "You can use it if you want. Just mention our name when you do—Earth and Sea. I really should be going. I've been here for an hour, going on and on. I hope I haven't been boring you. I tend to think that because I'm caught up in a subject, everyone else feels the same way."

"Not at all. I love this stuff. It's like an adventure novel. I had no idea. Before you go, I have to ask you again: Why were you interested in Howard Phelps?"

"He sold us out, like I told you, and we thought there might be evidence in his house."

"Your friend out there gets a bit carried away. Could he have gotten a bit overzealous in protecting you from a threat he saw in Phelps?"

Her eyes flashed. "I never met the man! I only saw him in class! I was just carrying out an assignment. We're organized like an army. I mean, we do what we're told. Trog is excitable, but not violent in the way you mean. He's as gentle as a lamb."

"Yeah, a three-hundred-pound lamb. And, by the way, what's with the name, Trog?"

"It's really Irving Gotlieb. He thought Trog sounded more romantic and . . . you know . . . environmental."

She got up to leave, and I motioned for Mrs. Meyers to remain seated. She had inadvertently gotten me out of a dicey situation. The least I could do was to read her rough draft. "I'll go over your work, then walk you to your car."

"Why, thank you, professor." She flashed me a big smile.

I stood up and shook Mara's hand.

"I owe you an article, too, Professor Martindale. I did take that seminar for credit."

I walked her to the door. "I'll look forward to reading it."

I spent the next hour going over Edna Ruth Meyers's first draft. Despite my earlier fears, it wasn't all that bad.

14

WEDNESDAY, APRIL 22

I COULDN'T SEEM TO CONCENTRATE on work the next morning, so I decided to organize my thoughts. Who were the key players here? I wrote them down on 3x5 index cards I sometimes used for library research.

Susan Foster: marine scientist, whale numbers, important to reputation, promotion & tenure. Motive to kill: jealousy, bitterness, the need to protect her research?

Minister Nagamo: Japanese fisheries minister, wanted high whale numbers to allow continued whaling, vital to important elements of country (big fishing companies, politicians from fishing area), his political future? Motive to kill: stop numbers from going public, influence final total, revenge for double-cross (Phelps as Japanese agent), blackmail gone wrong. [Note: Nagamo would keep hands clean, Jima would do dirty work. Who is Jima?]

John Strong, Marine Center director: substitutes new numbers fairly quickly after they turn up; how did they turn up. What motive did he have to change: financial, professional?

Eskimo delegates: trying to hold their own in world they think stacked against them, need high numbers to continue whaling, need to show constituents they are effective to stay in office and continue to get perks (pinstriped suits, travel, etc.). Motive to kill: influence numbers, stop release of numbers.

Mara & Trog: Earth and Sea members, semiradical environmental group, needing publicity, remove a perceived enemy. Motive to kill: revenge for all whales killed in past, protect undercover people?

Andy Kirk's father: wealthy, intelligent, brokenhearted, strong enough to kill someone (?), nothing to do with whales or the university. Motive to kill: revenge for death of son, leading son "astray" (Phelps as homosexual predator).

Scott Szabo: marine biology grad student, former lover of Phelps (?), on board Japanese ship, relationship with Susan (?), relationship with Andy K. (?). Motive to kill: anger over Phelps's sabotage of his fellowship application.

What now? Absentmindedly, I shuffled the seven cards as if I were about to play a hand of solitaire. My ruminations were suddenly interrupted by the ringing of the telephone.

"Hello."

"Good morning, Tom. It's Angela Pride of the Oregon State Police, Newport district. Is this a decent time to talk or am I interrupting something."

"No sergeant, I can talk. Anything new on the case?"

"I wanted you to know that your friend Ms. Foster appeared before the grand jury yesterday. We'll probably know about any indictment by tomorrow. She's back in her cell and could probably use a friend like you about now. If you want to go over there, I can get you in."

"What about the sheriff? He's practically banned me from the jail."

"Kutler can't do that, at least not technically. He's a big bluff sometimes. He makes value judgments about guilt or innocence too often. I guess he did that with Ms. Foster. At any rate,

I happen to know that he's down in L.A. at a law enforcement seminar until Friday. He won't be anywhere near the jail, if you want to get in. I'll clear it."

"Great. It sounds like you've made just the opposite value judgment about her." Her silence on the other end of the line seemed to confirm my thought. "I need your help on something else, sergeant. I've been sitting here sorting out all the people who have a part in my article, I mean the major players in the whole whaling controversy."

Sergeant Pride chuckled. She probably knew exactly where I was going with this.

"Yeah? Who are we talking about, and what do you want to know?" She had guessed. Was I that transparent?

"Okay. Is there any way for you to dig up some background on some people who were at the conference and may know something about the death of Howard Phelps?"

"Give me the names, and I'll see what I can do."

"Minister Nagamo and his aide Mr. Jima—big guy who looks like a sumo wrestler. I think he's the bodyguard."

"I'll try Interpol and check with an old friend in State Department security. Next?"

"The delegates from the Alaska Eskimo Whaling Commission. Damon Istook is the chief of the delegation. There were a lot of other men and women with him. I didn't talk to them. All I remember is lots of long, dark hair and ivory jewelry."

"And nice pinstriped suits."

"It's a status thing. They think they need to dress that way to keep up with the government bureaucrats and slick lobbyists they have to deal with in Washington."

"Anyone else?"

"Yes. I was visited last night by two fairly weird people from Earth and Sea, that semiradical environmental group. They're also in my class."

"How can you be semiradical?"

"What I mean by that is they're not real bomb throwers like some other organizations. But they're pretty determined to preserve the world and all the creatures in it. Anyway, their names are Mara and Trog."

"Trog?"

"Yeah. It's a pseudonym for Irving Gotlieb. He seems to be mute. Didn't say a thing, but beat me around a bit to protect her. He's like that character Lenny in *Of Mice and Men*.

"Who? Does this Lenny have a last name?"

"No. Concentrate on Irving Gotlieb. Forget Lenny. This Mara is a little thing with a slightly spacey air to her. She got into trouble outside the Marine Center the other day for spitting on two Japanese women. She's smart and knows a lot about what these environmental groups have done to protect whales."

"Yeah. Most of the time they don't mind if they break the law. We get 'em in here from time to time. Not too often. Our Eugene office handles most of that in this state. Aging hippies and their children who took up causes like whales after the Vietnam War ended. Anyone else?"

"One more name: Scott Szabo, another grad student. He's in my class, too. He was also at the scene of the death of another student last year that was never completely resolved. He could have been involved in Phelps's murder."

"Consider it done," replied Sergeant Pride. "I'll get back to you as soon as I can. Now, do you want to visit Ms. Foster?"

"Oh yes, very much. I appreciate that too. I'll be there around eleven."

〜 〜 〜

Susan Foster looked even more tired and haggard than when I had last seen her. Her orange jail jumpsuit was faded and threadbare, no doubt the result of too many washings in the county jail laundry. She wore no makeup and her hair was tied tightly behind her head.

"Tom. Thanks for coming." She sighed deeply. "It means a lot to me that you came. No one else has, except my attorney. So much for friends and colleagues standing by in time of trouble and all that. Everyone at the center seems to think I did it. Even people I considered good friends."

"It probably isn't that. It's just that some academics only care about how something helps or hurts. Will their careers be adversely affected if they are seen coming in here? What will their chairman think or the dean? How about students and their parents? The hypocrisy of it all makes me sick!"

"I'm sure I'll be indicted. The authorities think they've got me nailed—cold. Nothing like a bloody hammer and a missing report to do one in. I hadn't seen any of that stuff before, but they don't believe me. And no one seems to have figured out how I could drag his body from there to the cove and lift it into that whale's mouth. It defies logic, but nothing about any of this makes any sense to me."

"I've been looking around here and there and have come up with a few things."

I leaned forward conspiratorially. I couldn't touch her across the table, but I didn't want the guard outside the door to hear what I had to say. "Is it safe to talk? I mean this place isn't bugged, is it?"

"Oh, Tom, I don't think so. We're not in a *1984*-type situation—yet. Just keep your voice down."

"Howard Phelps had several secrets that could have gotten him killed. As I mentioned the other day, I am fairly certain he was involved sexually with both Andy Kirk and Scott Szabo."

"Andy, maybe, but not Scott. That's impossible!"

Her answer surprised me. "Why impossible with Scott and not Andy?"

"Well . . . I . . . as I said before, there were only rumors about Howard being gay. Nothing about him being involved sexually with these two students or any other students. Anyway, I've always felt that kind of thing was his own business."

"Yeah," I replied. "True. But all that sanctity of private life stuff goes out the window when it comes to playing around with students. Even tenure doesn't protect you in that case."

"That and stealing money are really the only things that can get a fully tenured faculty member fired," she said. "You can be a lousy teacher and a bad researcher and a total son of a bitch and still keep your job. But not if you fool around with your students."

"But it does happen."

"Sure. Of course. Many male professors at this university and a lot of other places leave their wives and children after falling in love with a female student. It all depends on the age of the student in question and the circumstances. If you flaunt it, you're dead. If it's discreet and the old wife and the girl's parents don't complain, you're probably in the clear."

"What about when the student is male?"

"The whole character of the situation changes. Now it's dirty old man taking advantage of innocent young male student. No matter how the student behaves or eggs the professor on, they're supposed to ignore it and recommend that the student seek counseling."

"I think that happened with Howard and Andy and Howard and Scott."

"Howard was a fussy bachelor type—never married, never seemed to be interested in women, devoted only to work. I only really knew him professionally. I never saw him socially. No one did. Andy Kirk was a cute kid—nice looking, clean cut, a good personality—and very smart, although he didn't do all that well in the graduate program. I guess it's possible if you look for it. I guess, I never did."

"I talked to his father and it all seems to fit. Here's my scenario: Howard takes Andy on as an assistant, becomes infatuated with him. Andy responds in kind, either because he reciprocates or sees that a close personal relationship with the good professor will help his academic career or a combination of both. One gets tired of the other—or someone else threatens to blow the whistle. Anyway, it's broken off, and they go on the cruise on the Japanese ship and, next thing everyone knows, Andy Kirk falls overboard, his body never found. I'm not sure how it escalated to murder."

"I guess it's plausible," Susan said, staring into space. "Really sad, if it is true. Howard was my mentor. Of course, he never was interested in me romantically—wrong sex, I guess, if what you say is true. But he was very helpful at first. Showed me the ropes, how to avoid mistakes he said he'd made. Until recently . . ."

"When you suddenly became a rival?"

"Yeah, maybe. I don't know. I didn't see it. I thought he was always trying to spur me on to greater heights. 'I'm only doing this for your own good'—that kind of thing."

"I've read the report of the investigation of Andy's accident. It was pretty perfunctory."

"That's probably because John Strong did it. He would want to get it over with fast, not to hide anything but to contain the damage to the university and to the people involved."

"He was successful. The incident was barely reported, as I recall. How much do you trust Strong? Is he your friend in all of this?"

"I've never had any reason to think otherwise. He runs a good center and tries to keep the scientists and the administrators in Corvallis happy. But he is a bottom line kind of guy. He'd want to get it all over with—Kirk's death, I mean—and move on."

It was time to lower the boom—to change my good cop into a decidedly bad one.

"I mentioned that I'd read the report about the accident. You can imagine my surprise at finding your name on the manifest of those on board the Japanese ship. Didn't you think I was entitled to know that you were there? Didn't you realize I'd find out? Why lie about it? How do you think it makes me feel? I've been spending a lot of my time trying to get you out of this mess. Wasn't I entitled to the truth?"

I was really getting angry, so I got up and walked to the window as I tried to calm down. I had kept my voice low to keep the ubiquitous matron from barging through the door. I glanced at Susan and saw that she had started to cry. I didn't move to her side this time, but stayed where I was.

"I made a big mistake on that ship, and I didn't want you to find out."

"What kind of mistake? A trifling thing like shove Andy Kirk overboard?" I seemed to be transforming myself into Mr. Hyde.

She turned her red-rimmed eyes toward me, a shocked look on her face. "How could you even think that? Why would I kill Andy Kirk?"

I resumed my seat across from her, still too steamed to do anything but glare at her.

"What mistake did you make, Susan? What mistake were you so afraid to tell me about?"

She looked me right in the face and cleared her throat before answering. "I had a little too much to drink the night Andy disappeared, and I slept with Scott Szabo."

I slammed my hand on the table—hard. Surprisingly, the matron did not come running.

"Who seduced who?" My voice suddenly got very cold. I was feeling detached from the scene.

"I guess we both felt a mutual attraction. He's very good looking, and I was feeling lonely and sorry for myself. It . . . just . . . happened. I'm not proud of myself, and I don't think the seduction of a graduate student would look all that good in my promotion dossier."

"Did it ever occur to you that he was using you? I mean, he used Phelps, too. Hell, he's even making moves on me—at least I think so. That guy'll do anything to advance his career!"

"Nothing else has happened since. We agreed to keep our little escapade to ourselves."

"Did he ask you to do anything else for him?"

"I wrote him a letter of recommendation for a fellowship he applied for in New Zealand."

I was aghast that she didn't see any connection. "Didn't you know that Phelps declined to recommend him for the same thing? So he turned to his old bed partner for help!"

"Tom! That remark is not worthy of you. You're reacting for reasons that go beyond this case. And besides, he didn't get the fellowship."

I couldn't deny that there was a kernel of truth in what she said. She and Szabo had been intimate in a way that she and I never had, but I'd never admit it. It felt better to let my wounded pride prevail.

"What does that have to do with anything?" I said. "You still don't get it, do you? Something else: did Phelps know about your little 'escapade,' as you call it?"

She hung her head. "He mentioned it once in passing. He said he wouldn't hold it against me in deciding on my promotion."

"God, this just gets worse and worse. Don't you see, if he said that, it's precisely what he planned to do? Maybe he was going to tie it into making sure you came up with the right figures in your research, figures that the Japanese—his old patrons—would like. This gives you a very good motive for murdering him. This will probably come out in the investigation. This is really bad, Sue, really bad."

I stood up abruptly.

"Tom, please don't react this way. I need you." She reached for my hand, but I pulled it away.

"I've got to be going."

"Are you going to abandon me, Tom?"

I couldn't look at her. "I don't know."

Silence permeated the room.

"I might as well ask what you know about the other students on the voyage." She looked at me hopefully. "I'm not saying I'm planning to do anything with the information, but at least I'll have a name in case I decide to help."

"Anna Garcia left the university right after the accident," she said quietly. "She was a promising grad student who had a merit scholarship. She just left. Didn't even go back to class. Moved out of her apartment. No one has heard from her since. She was from California, I think. Maybe she's there."

"I don't remember seeing any testimony from her in the Strong report. Maybe I'll look into it."

"Dear Tom. I'd hate to lose you over this . . . this . . . what did they call it in Victorian novels—dalliance."

"It sounds like it was far from that!" I wasn't smiling. I felt betrayed by all of this.

She stood up. The guard opened the door and walked toward us. Sue took my hands in hers and squeezed. This time, I didn't pull away, although I was tempted.

"Don't desert me, Tom."

She mouthed a "please," tears welling up in her eyes, as the guard led her back through the steel door at the other end of the room. As always, her keys were jangling as she walked.

15

I DECIDED I HAD TO KEEP TRYING to help Susan, no matter how I felt. She had kept things from me, but I couldn't abandon her now.

That afternoon, I drove to the main university campus. I hadn't been in my Corvallis office for over a month, and I needed to check my mail. I also planned to try finding Anna Garcia.

My trip was over Oregon Highway 20, a one-hour drive from Newport when weather and traffic cooperated. The highway goes through some of the loveliest terrain in the state: hillsides covered with tall Douglas firs, lush ferns and wild flowers near the roadway, even an occasional waterfall cascading off the rocks in the wet season. It was not uncommon to see deer crossing the road or grazing among cattle to camouflage themselves in meadows in the middle of the Coast Range.

Of course, the drive wasn't all beauty and serenity. You could often see one or two deer carcasses on the drive, victims of the erratic log trucks and chip trucks that sometimes went so fast they rolled over on curves that their drivers had misjudged. Then, there were the clear-cuts—whole hillsides where the trees had been cut down, with only stumps remaining. It was a devastating sight. I could never understand why timber companies couldn't seem to fathom the damage these clear-cuts did to their images.

Sure, they ran high-visibility PR campaigns about their replanting of seedlings. One of my former students had even gotten a job that included producing a TV spot of the process. It was a good production, but I still didn't totally believe the premise, and I still found it dumb that the companies devastated everything in the paths of their chain saws, then tried to convince everyone later that it was beneficial.

This was at least one instance where environmentalists like Mara weren't exaggerating.

I was making good time and would probably get to campus by three P.M. or so—just in time to get my campus mail I hoped would include Anna's current address. I had called a friend in the registrar's office for help, and she had promised to look it up. I was lucky because such information is usually not available to someone who isn't that student's professor, and never to anyone on the outside.

As usual, I had to concentrate on the road so much that I didn't look beyond it very often, even at the scenery. It was a constant battle to pass slow campers and log trucks without taking chances. I had long ago resigned myself to being patient until I reached one of the few passing lanes.

After the wide spot in the road called Eddyville, I noticed that a white station wagon seemed to be taking a lot of chances to stay one car behind me. He—or she—would pass on curves and even in narrow spots to keep that position. Because the vehicle immediately behind me was a pickup truck riding fairly high off the ground, I could never get a good look at my pursuer—if indeed it was a pursuer.

I was probably imagining it anyway. My encounter with the guys in the blue van had made me more than a little paranoid. I drove the rest of the way somewhat concerned that I was being followed, but there was very little I could do about it.

The journalism department was located on the second floor of the south wing of Agriculture Hall, a hulk of a building constructed in 1909. Despite its age, the building was a wonderful structure, with wide halls and high ceilings. Although the desks with inkwells in the upper corner and seventy years of carved initials had been replaced with more modern, if less interesting, models, the rooms still had some wonderful features. One room that I regularly taught in had a blackboard on ropes and pulleys that allowed the user to raise it, revealing an identical blackboard underneath. Another room contained two ancient horseshoe-shaped copy desks pushed together to make a great seminar table.

For my office, I had scrounged around to get two wooden filing cabinets and three great oak chairs. Although they didn't match, they were very much in keeping with the age of the building as a whole. I had to settle for a more pedestrian wooden desk with a black slate top, however, because the chairman appropriated the roll-top for himself. It all made for a nice office anyway.

It was to this domain that I was now headed, crossing the large expanse of land named, appropriately enough, the Library Quad. Our building was next to the library. Students were making their way up the walk into that building as I crossed the diagonal path of the quad. As usual, the lights were on, illuminating the stacks of books behind the glass front of the structure—a real temple of knowledge that most people don't appreciate. For my part, I couldn't imagine a world without books, and I intended to spend the rest of my working life writing them.

My daydreams about the glory of knowledge were interrupted by loud talking coming from a group of students walking up to the library's front door. At their center, laughing and talking the loudest, was Scott Szabo. When he saw me notice him, he quickly turned his head, pretending not to see me. I continued my stroll into Ag Hall and walked up the stairs to my office on the second floor. It was four thirty when I put my key in the lock of the door. Not many people were around this late in the day. The department was deserted.

My friend had come through with a listing for Anna Garcia's permanent residence, I learned via a message on my answer machine. Apparently she lived with a sister in Salinas, California. I dialed the number right away, wondering in the back of my mind how I could afford—or justify to myself—a trip to Salinas.

"*Hola*. Garcia residence."

"Is this the home of Anna Garcia?"

"It might be. Who wants to know?"

As a reporter, I had always been amazed at how much people would tell me over the phone. It was an important tool, if you used it right. You had to sound sincere and nonthreatening. It wouldn't do to seem abrupt or pushy. After all, I was interrupting whoever it was on the other end of the line, in this case a youngish sounding woman. I certainly needed her more than she needed me.

"I'm one of her professors at the university." A little white lie never hurt anyone—for the greater good, I always told myself. "I am trying to locate her. She left school so fast last year, I didn't get her address. I just wondered how she was doing and if she planned to return to school."

"That depends on why you want to know."

"I'm just concerned, that's all. Nothing more."

Another white lie, but it was for a good cause.

"You better talk to my mother."

"*Hola*. Is this Anna's professor?" asked her mother, with a tone of respect and friendliness in her voice. People who aren't

used to talking with college professors often give them the def-
erence usually accorded a priest or minister. They seem to think
we should be held in awe, just because we have gone to college
a bit longer than most.

"Good afternoon, *Señora* Garcia. My name is Thomas
Martindale. I teach at the university." Just as I said that, I glanced
toward the hall and caught a glimpse of someone placing his
head against the frosted glass of my door, then move away. Was
the door locked? I strained to see, then decided it was. I was
right in the middle of my call, so I ignored whoever it was.

"I'm trying to reach Anna. It's nothing bad, but I need to talk
to her."

"About her schooling?"

"Yes . . . in a manner of speaking. Yes. About a class she took
last year."

Another stretch of the truth. She had been in a course, it just
wasn't my course.

"I am sorry to say that she has dropped out for now. But she
will return. She is earning some money by working in a restaurant. We are not rich, Professor Martin. She is the first in our
family to go to the university. We are very proud."

"I know you are. And you should be. Is she working there in
Salinas?"

"Oh, no. Not here."

"Oh, I see. Where is she working?"

"She is still in Oregon. In Eugene. Do you know that city?"

"Yes. It is near to where I am now." I could hardly believe my
good luck. Eugene was only forty miles south of Corvallis.
There would be no worry about the time and money to fly to
California.

"What is the restaurant? The name, I mean?"

"Just a moment, please."

She turned away from the phone and shouted to someone in Spanish. The shadow at the door was gone. I glanced at my watch. Six P.M. I could still get to Eugene tonight.

"Professor. Are you still there?"

"Yes, *Señora* Garcia. I'm here."

"I have the name and number. It is called the Ambrosia. Have you heard of it?"

"Yes. I've even eaten there."

The Ambrosia was one of those good restaurants with a rich hippie look—oak furniture, stained glass, ferns—housed in a building that used to be a fine home. The food was good. A nice place, if a bit pretentious at times. *Señora* Garcia gave me the number.

"Thank you very much for your help."

"It was my pleasure, professor. It is an honor to talk to one of Anna's college teachers. Please tell her I love her and to write to me soon."

"I will do that, *señora*, I'll be happy to do it. Thank you again and goodbye."

How easy it is to stretch the truth and get what you want. I quickly dialed the Ambrosia's number.

"Good evening, Ambrosia."

"Is Anna Garcia working tonight?"

"Yes, but she doesn't come on until six thirty. She has the late shift."

"I didn't want to talk to her. I wanted to make a reservation and be seated in her section. I've heard she's a very good waitress."

"We prefer to call our people 'servers.' What time did you want to come in?"

"How about nine?"

"How many people in your party?"

"Just one."

"Name please."

"Tom Martin-da . . . Martin. Tom Martin."

"We'll see you at nine, Mr. Martin."

That done, I decided to go through my mail in the time I had before I left. It was the usual mixture of departmental memos, university newsletters, textbook brochures, and a few free books. I would be on four committees next fall, two of them in the department, two at the university level. Universities really functioned just below the higher echelons through a series of committees. That meant the institution could hire fewer people, what with faculty members needing to do committee service as one of the criteria for promotion and tenure. It was a rather inefficient system, one that spread the blame and usually delayed action on even the important things. But it had its consolations because the chairman usually did all the work, convening meetings only when a vote was needed. If you weren't chairman, you only had to show up. If you cared enough to put in the time, you could maneuver yourself into the chair slot anyway.

My course list for next year was there, too. Eight courses over three terms with one course down the next winter so I could start work on a book. Not a bad life, really. I liked the campus atmosphere and the chance to work with the kids. We weren't as big as the University of Oregon School of Journalism, but our students were just as good. I liked to think that we gave them a better education because of our smaller size. They got more attention and the chance to do writing that gets published.

Someone tried the door again. The shadowy figure had returned, although I didn't see any movement this time through the frosted glass. The guy in the white station wagon? Scott Szabo? I felt jumpy enough not to want to find out on my own. I picked up the phone and dialed campus security. A woman answered after one ring.

"This is Professor Martindale in Journalism. I don't mean to seem jittery, but someone has been lurking around my office. Could someone come by and check it out? Good . . . and, Miss? Tell them to make a lot of noise as they come in. Yes, I'm in Ag Hall, room two twenty-three."

No sound now, either inside or out. I felt safe up here, although I did pull the blind. It was nearly seven thirty by now and almost dark. I fiddled around some more in my office, straightening up files and books on the shelves. I resorted my mail, keeping what I would need and placing it in a saved file. I even dusted my desk.

Where were those guys? I don't suppose they were as skilled as regular cops. Institutions never got the best policemen or the best doctors. It was pay, I guess. Did it apply to writing professors, too? I didn't want to answer that.

This was getting ridiculous. I hadn't heard anything from the hall for a long time. I was getting out of here and driving to Eugene. I'd miss my reservation if I didn't leave now. I turned out the lights in my office. Then I opened the door and stuck my head out fast, before drawing it back. I'd seen that in police movies and it seemed to make sense as a technique. All the lights were out in the hall, even the exit sign down the hall over the stairwell—an ominous sign.

My shoes made more noise than I would have preferred, as I walked quickly down the long and wide hall. All the offices were dark on either side. It was lucky I had trod these ancient boards so often the past ten years; I knew my way, but it was a bit spooky. I remembered the bat that lived three stories up and hoped his nocturnal hunts had taken him elsewhere tonight.

Just as I opened the fire door to go into the stairway itself, I fell over something. With nothing to break my fall, I landed hard on all fours, tearing the knee of one pants leg in the process.

Feeling like I'd been pushed, I braced for a blow to the head from my unseen assailant. Then, my heart nearly stopped as I shined my penlight on what had caused me to fall. The security guard who had been sent to retrieve me lay just behind me.

16

THE GUARD HAD A STRONG PULSE, and I couldn't feel any blood as I touched his head.

"Are you all right?"

"What . . . what happened?"

"You were hit on the head. Don't try to stand up. Lean against the wall for a minute. Have you got a radio to call this in?"

"Yeah, I think so," he said, fumbling in his coat pocket. "Who are you?"

"Tom Martindale. I'm the guy who called for help. I think the bad guys are gone now. If you'll be all right, I've got to leave."

I didn't wait for a response as I headed down the stairs. Talk about ungrateful. I was leaving a man who had come here to help me. But I was late for my appointment in Eugene. And, besides, I had concluded, fairly cold-heartedly, that help was on the way. The staccato bursts from his radio I heard when I reached the bottom confirmed that hope. He would be fine.

No one seemed to be following me as I left Corvallis. To make sure, I went south and then doubled back north several times, checking in my rearview mirror constantly for a white station wagon—or a blue van. As a last precaution, I drove to Eugene by the more remote route along Peoria Road.

My drive was uneventful. I didn't see a car behind me until I got to Junction City. Thus emboldened, I drove the rest of the way on Highway 99W.

I arrived at the Ambrosia at nine P.M. Not bad for all the hassles of the night. I always considered myself some kind of interloper in Eugene. Part of it was the rivalry between the two universities and their journalism programs. Part of it was that I always felt kind of out of place here. Everyone around the university and restaurants like this looked like they were out of a 1960s time warp: beads, beards, patchouli oil, and Birkenstock sandals.

The interior of the restaurant was pleasant and reassuring. After the kind of day I had had, I needed some solace. I was looking forward to a good meal, and I had dressed up for the occasion with a blue blazer, and a special tie—a yellow number with blue peace symbols on it—homage to the peaceniks who called Eugene home. Only the tear in my pants marred my preppy look.

I was seated by a young woman wearing a long floral dress and, of course, Birkenstocks. "Enjoy." She handed me the large menu. "Your server will be Anna."

Good. Something was working out.

A busboy in a white coat filled my water glass and placed a basket of bread on the table. He smiled but said nothing. Then a beautiful girl approached my table. She was tall and slim, with dark curly hair and great teeth.

"Good evening. I'm Anna, your server. Do you want to start with a cocktail or wine?"

"Hello. Yes. I'll have a glass of house red wine. And I already know what I want. Grilled prawns with rice and Caesar salad."

"That's what I like. Someone who knows what they want." She smiled and departed.

No need to scare her by pouncing all over her with questions. There were few patrons at this late hour. I'd enjoy my meal and then ask her to sit down while I had my coffee. The meal was excellent.

Anna Garcia brought the dessert tray and a pot of coffee. "Black?"

"Yes. I'll have that . . . is it apple cobbler?"

"Apple torte with demiglaze and almond slivers."

"Oh, I should have known."

She returned with the dessert.

"Anna. You don't know me, but I know who you are."

The look of alarm that swept across her face was palpable. She set the plate on the table so hard a fork fell to the floor.

"Don't be alarmed. I just want to ask you something."

She relaxed, but was still frowning.

"Is it possible for you to sit down for a minute? It's less awkward to talk."

She eased down in the chair opposite me.

"My name is Tom Martindale. I teach journalism at the university in Corvallis."

She sighed and her apprehension seemed to melt away.

"I'm a friend of Susan Foster in marine biology. I believe you took a course from her in the last year or so?"

"Oh, yes. Professor Foster. Very nice lady and a good teacher. I read about her trouble in the paper."

"That's why I'm here. She didn't kill Professor Phelps. I'm trying to help her out. I believe you were a friend of Andy Kirk?"

"Yeah. Another tragedy. Andy was killed . . . I mean drowned last year."

"That's why I'm really here, Anna. You took that course with Professor Phelps and were on that voyage last year. I mean the one where Andy was swept overboard."

"Yes, but I don't know anything about it."

"Then why did you leave school?"

"I was low on money. My scholarship wasn't renewed. Grades, you know. Professor Phelps said he'd help me."

"It sounds as though he didn't come through with that promise."

"No, he didn't. I told him I didn't see anything that night, but he wouldn't believe me."

Anna then started to sob. Luckily by then, all the other diners had left except for one couple in a side room who seemed not to notice. The hostess, the busboy, and a tall male waiter came running over.

"Anna. Is everything all right?"

"Is this guy bothering you?"

"No, no. I'm fine. May I have some of your water, Professor Martindale?"

I nodded, and she took several fast gulps. The others retreated, skeptically. I waited for her to calm down as the rest of them busied themselves in other parts of the room, but kept my table in sight. Anna was someone everyone obviously liked and cared about.

"Feeling better? Can you talk some more?"

"Sure. If I can help Professor Foster, that would be great."

"You said Professor Phelps didn't believe you when you said you didn't see anything. What did you mean?"

"I was on that Japanese ship as an observer with Professor Phelps and all the other kids. I couldn't sleep that night—the night Andy got lost—so I was out in the passageway when I saw Professor Phelps go into Andy's cabin."

"I thought he had another male student in with him."

"No, that's what the story in the paper said, but Professor Phelps put Scott into another cabin at the last minute."

"Scott Szabo was not Andy Kirk's cabin mate?"

"No, he wasn't. Do you know Scott? He became Mr. Phelps's assistant after Andy . . . a . . . disappeared."

"I've met Scott, yeah. Did Professor Phelps give any reason for the change in cabin arrangements?"

"He said he wanted Andy in a single room so they could go over research notes and stuff during the trip."

"Was there anything else going on between them, Anna, I mean besides work?"

"Like what?"

"Like sex."

Her face reddened.

"I . . . don't . . . know."

"I know that Andy was gay, Anna. That's nothing to be ashamed of. What's bad is that Professor Phelps seems to have taken advantage of Andy, by putting a lot of pressure on him that had nothing to do with training him to be a marine biologist."

"Yeah. Andy told me a lot of stuff. When we first met, I hoped something would develop between us."

"You mean romantically?"

"Yes. I flirted with him a lot. We went to the movies and out for coffee a few times. After a while, when he didn't kiss me good night, I thought there was something wrong with me, so I asked him. Then he told me that he liked me as a friend, but had no interest in me romantically. He told me he was gay. He hadn't, as they say, come out yet, but he was attracted only to men."

"How did Phelps come into this? Did Andy tell you they were involved?"

"He said Professor Phelps had propositioned him a few months after he became his research assistant. He had been thrilled by the attention from this older man, a man he admired and wanted to pattern his life after."

"Did anyone else know?"

"Not that I ever saw. I never mentioned it to anyone. Andy was a good friend, and I didn't want to hurt him. I don't like gossip. It seems like kids have always whispered about me behind my back. I hated it, but I learned to hold my head up high and ignore them. I wanted Andy to do that with his homosexuality, but he was too afraid, mostly of his father, I think."

"Did you see Scott Szabo or Professor Foster up and around that night?"

She hesitated and lowered her head.

"What you know may help us find out what happened to Andy."

"Like I said, I hate to gossip, but I saw what I saw."

"And that was . . ."

"An hour or so before I met Andy in the passageway, I saw Scott go into Professor Foster's cabin. I thought maybe she was helping him with his research or something, but he never came out, as far as I know."

"I doubt they were looking at slides through a microscope," I said cynically.

She blushed and turned away. I felt my face get red too, a reaction that made me mad at myself. Right then, I vowed not to care about any of this. What Susan Foster did in her private life was of no concern to me. I pushed ahead in getting Anna to continue her story.

"What else happened that night?'

"I heard voices coming from Andy's cabin—he and Professor Phelps. I peeked out and then Andy ran out, and I let him see me."

"Where was Phelps?"

"I could see him naked on one of the bunks as the door opened for a moment, then slammed shut."

"So, what did Andy say to you?"

"He just brushed by me and pressed something in my hand. He said something like, 'This guy is bleeding me dry. I can't stand him to touch me anymore. Keep this and use it if you have to.' Then he ran down the passageway and up on deck, I guess. I never saw him again."

"What did he give you, Anna?"

She walked over to the sideboard and got her purse. "It was this," she said when she returned. "It's Andy's lucky piece. Professor Phelps gave it to him when they first . . . um . . . got together. It's called scrimshaw. The whalers used to etch drawings onto whale ivory in a special way to pass the time on long voyages. The scenes were usually of ships or whales or other marine mammals."

The smooth white object she handed to me was beautiful: a Gray whale being pursued by what looked like a small boat filled with men holding harpoons. I say "looked like" because this scrimshaw had apparently been cut in half with a chisel. Parts of the scene were missing. One of its four sides was rough.

"What happened to the rest of this?"

"He said it had been Professor Phelps's favorite piece of scrimshaw. I guess he collects . . . collected . . . it. When he and Andy got involved, he deliberately cut it in half and kept the other part himself. He said it was a sign of affection and a symbol of their relationship, or something like that."

"So Andy wanted to get rid of it as another sign—that everything was over between them?"

"I guess so."

"What do you think he meant by 'use it if you have to'?"

"I guess to tell someone about Professor Phelps, if anything happened to him. To tell what Dr. Phelps was really like."

"Did he think something was going to happened to him?"

"He didn't have time to say anything more. He was really scared, Mr. Martindale. I could see it in his eyes."

"What happened next?"

"Andy said he needed some air and was going on deck. I stayed in the shadows and watched the door. After a few minutes, Professor Phelps came out of the cabin buttoning up his shirt and pulling on a parka. Then he ran down the passageway toward where Andy had gone."

"Did he see you?"

"No, I didn't let him. I ran to my cabin and locked the door after that."

"Did you ever tell anyone about what you saw or about the scrimshaw?"

"Nobody. I didn't want to tarnish Andy's memory. I considered the scrimshaw a part of him. I've treasured it."

"Did Phelps know you had it?"

"No. I certainly didn't want to tell him. He'd have tried to get it."

"So, how did you happen to tell him you hadn't seen anything?"

"Oh, that. After Andy was reported missing, the professor called us all together in his cabin to tell us what happened. We were in our bathrobes."

"Did Professor Foster and Scott come in together?"

"I'm not sure. When I got to the cabin, everyone else was already there. Anyway, after Professor Phelps finished telling us about Andy, he said, as an afterthought, did anyone lose a bathrobe sash in the hall. He held one up. By the color, it was apparent to everyone that it was mine, so I couldn't deny it. I claimed it and he gave it to me."

"Did he confront you about that?"

"Not then. But a week after we got back, he called me into his office and asked me point-blank where I had been and what I had seen. I denied seeing anything. Said I'd been on the way to the head. But I don't think he believed me."

"So, when did he bring up about helping you?"

"In the same conversation. Real smooth, without batting an eye, he changed the subject. He asked me if I needed help in getting another merit scholarship. He'd help me, if I helped him. As I said before, he never did."

"Did he specify what you'd be helping him about?"

"No, I think it was understood what he meant. I sure understood."

"Did he ever mention the scrimshaw to you—or anyone?"

"No. If he was worried about it, he never let on. Of course, he didn't know I had it."

"Boy, Anna. I must be exhausting you. I didn't mean to make this into a third degree kind of thing. I can't thank you enough. You've really been helpful. I appreciate it. Susan Foster will appreciate it. The more I find out about Howard Phelps, the more I'm finding that there were a lot of people who disliked him more than she did. He was a very nasty man. From what you know of him, do you think he could have pushed Andy overboard?"

"I don't know. If he was afraid of being exposed, maybe he did get that desperate."

I patted her hand. "Thanks a lot. I hope you'll come back to school. You know they've got a lot of scholarships for minority students. I'll have the financial aid office send you a flier, if you want. I'd be glad to write you a letter of recommendation, if that would help. Please apply. You need to come back. You don't want to work here for the rest of your life."

"You can say that again. I'd appreciate it. Thanks."

After I paid the bill and tipped Anna, I got up and offered my hand to Anna. Instead of shaking it, she placed the scrimshaw in my palm.

"You take it, Professor Martindale. Maybe you'll find the other half. Maybe it will help you figure out what happened. Maybe it will bring you good luck."

17

THURSDAY, APRIL 23

THE NEXT MORNING, BACK HOME IN CORVALLIS, I ate breakfast at seven thirty and headed west out of town on Highway 20. The trip was uneventful and there wasn't much traffic, except for the log trucks that were already on the road.

Ten miles or so past Eddyville, I glanced in my rearview mirror and my heart sank. The white station wagon was several vehicles back. I immediately felt my stomach do a flip flop and I began feeling nauseated. I was also getting mad.

I stepped on the gas of my little Ford Escort, determined to get away from my pursuer. I rounded a corner and noticed an unmarked county road on the right. I slowed the car just enough to make the turn safely and picked up speed as soon as I could. The road was paved but narrow with a dense thicket of ferns, salal, blackberry, and other wild plants growing to a height above the roof line of the car.

In five miles or so, the road got steeper and the pavement turned to gravel. At about that point, I passed a sign that read "Watch for Log Trucks." As if on cue, one of those huge vehicles loomed ahead of me. We both stopped, and the driver got out and walked toward my car. He leaned in to talk to me.

"Been this way before, mister?" he asked above the rumble of his idling diesel engine.

He was young and friendly looking, wearing the typical lumberjack uniform: a gray striped work shirt, jeans held up by bright red suspenders, heavy boots, and a hard hat that looked like the helmets soldiers in World War I wore in the trenches.

"No. I hoped I was taking a shortcut."

"To where?"

"Oh, I guess Siletz and eventually Newport."

"Well, you're a little off course for Newport. It's back that way." He pointed in the direction I'd just come from. "Siletz is this way, but the road's kind of narrow and slow. You'd have better luck turning around and going back."

"Well . . . I . . . I want to get back in here to take some photos. I'm . . . I'm . . . a photographer. Nature stuff. Outdoors and all of that." Mr. Liar was surfacing again.

He took off his hat and smoothed his hair in apparent befuddlement at what this city slicker was telling him. He looked at the empty seat beside me.

"Camera's in the trunk," I answered his unasked question.

I love good photography and think I know what a good photo is, but I haven't taken a shot since my Instamatic days.

"Your choice. Just be careful of washouts. Pretty bad winter up here. Also, don't get off the road on foot or anything. Some of these valleys have got hippie marijuana growers living in them. They got booby traps and really mean dogs—so bad the state police won't go into some of them. Got that? I mean, be careful."

I nodded, weighing a return to the highway and the white station wagon or a venture ahead into unknown peril.

"I've got to get my load of logs to the mill over in Toledo. Mind if I ask you to back up to that last turnout? Easier for you than me."

"Oh, sure. Glad to. And thanks for the advice."

He nodded and strode back to his rig. As I backed up to the turnout, he gunned his engine, sending belches of black smoke out of the truck's twin exhaust pipes. When I was safely out of the way, he rolled his vehicle forward, pausing to wave and honk his air horn several times as he passed me.

I waved back and resumed my journey. The winding road made progress slow, and I worried about the damage the gravel would do to the paint on my car every time I had the chance to speed up. Fast or slow, my car raised big clouds of dust in its wake.

Several miles passed uneventfully, and I was actually beginning to enjoy the scenery. As the road climbed, the trees on the left fell away so I could look out across the mountains and see the Pacific Ocean in the distance. The road hugged the hillside on the right. I stopped at one point just to look at the view, forgetting for the moment that I was being pursued.

As I started down a long slope that curved to the left where the road entered dense forest, the white station wagon suddenly came into view in my side mirror.

"God. Not again!"

Who was this guy, and why was he following me? Maybe what I was finding out about Howard Phelps's murder was making somebody very nervous.

In spite of the bad road, I had to outrun my pursuer. But, in an Escort? I accelerated slightly and the car picked up speed going down the hill. I stayed as close to the cliff as possible to avoid the crumbling edge. Too late I realized that the heavy rains of the winter had washed away the road near the bottom. Too late I saw that the road I counted on to get me safely out of my predicament no longer existed.

My car wouldn't have flown any better if it had had wings. The momentum it gained going down the hill propelled it through the air like a ski jumper at Aspen. It would have been thrilling if I hadn't been so scared.

Miraculously, the car landed on all four wheels in a flat area that had once been a viewpoint. Feeling relieved to be alive, I sat for a second to take stock of my situation. Except for a nasty cut over my left eye, I seemed to be amazingly unscathed—no broken bones or erupting blood vessels. I would be awfully stiff and sore in the morning, but what else was new?

Sudden movement interrupted my reveries. Even though I had put on the emergency brake, the car was beginning to roll slowly toward the edge—and the deep canyon below. I ripped off my seatbelt, opened the door, and jumped out as quickly as I could, moving out of the way just as the car went quietly over the edge. Still aware that someone was probably watching all this from above, I ran into the woods. Once there, I paused to listen for the inevitable sound of metal and glass far below. Seconds later, the car hit bottom. I braced for the explosion of the gas tank but, miraculously, nothing happened. The last thing I needed was to start a forest fire.

From my vantage point in the trees, I had a good view up the road. At first I saw nothing. The station wagon was apparently obscured by the shelf-like outcropping that had once been the road. I heard stones falling and realized that this guy was making his way on foot down the high embankment where the road had washed out.

I moved back into the forest and started looking for a place to hide. I soon found a large fir tree next to a big mound of rocks. It was easy to climb into the tree from the rocks and then use the strong limbs to move higher and higher into the dense growth at the top. My fear of being caught overshadowed any worry about falling. I only hoped my movement didn't send pinecones falling on the head of whoever was after me.

After several minutes, I stopped to catch my breath and listen. Because of the thick tree limbs, I was fairly certain I couldn't be seen. The sound of falling stones had now been replaced by feet trampling heavily on the forest floor. The sound got closer and I held my breath, trying to look down without making a sound.

My pursuer stopped right below me and sat down on the large boulders I had used to climb up on to my present precarious perch. He fumbled in his pocket for something, but I dared not lean over too far to see. I waited motionlessly. Soon, wafts of smoke reached my nose. Just what I needed: a contemplative, pipe-smoking killer!

He sat there for over fifteen minutes. I taxed every muscle and bone in my body in an effort not to move. Luckily for me, a slight breeze came up so that the occasional sound of stirring leaves helped mask the thundering beat of my heart. I still didn't dare look down at him.

Suddenly, he got up and walked back to where the car had gone over the side into the ravine. I couldn't imagine that even he—super being that he seemed to be—would try to rappel to the bottom to find my car to see if my body was in it.

I listened carefully to his footsteps for another five minutes or so. They were getting more faint all the time. I decided I had to make my move. I climbed down slowly, branch by branch, until I reached the boulder that had acted as a stepladder when I went up. I scrambled down and started running in the opposite direction.

I'm not much of an athlete, but I've always been a pretty good runner. I made good time following what was probably a deer trail through the forest in what I thought was a westerly direction. After ten minutes, I slowed to a fast walk, then stopped to listen. At first I heard nothing but the noises of the forest. Then, in the distance, I heard the unmistakable sound of someone running hard toward me.

Just then I spotted a wire nearly covered by leaves and pine needles on the ground. I sidestepped it and changed directions, moving south to avoid it. Was it a trip wire set up by the marijuana growers the logger had warned me about?

I had read that Oregon had ideal conditions for growing pot; added to that was the relative isolation of the Coast Range. I had probably stumbled—almost—into one of those operations. I hoped my pursuer would blunder blindly ahead and get hung up in whatever that booby trap was set to do. I was so certain that he would, in fact, that I stopped to listen. In minutes I heard what sounded like a loud pop, followed by shouting from where the wire had been tripped.

I slowed to a walk, but kept moving away from the commotion. Soon, I came to the start of a high wire fence running west. This was obviously the limit of the pot grower's property. Why they hadn't fenced off the eastern boundary I could only guess.

I felt safer now. The guy who was after me was probably incapacitated and explaining his presence to the pot heads. The fence would also serve as a guide out of here. For good luck, I rubbed the scrimshaw piece in my pocket.

The forest was dense between the deer trail and the fence for a few miles, then thinned out. I stopped to peer into what was a small lush valley. In the distance at the bottom of the hill, I could see a log house with smoke rising out of its chimney. Very blissful, like the set for the *Lassie* or *Little House on the Prairie* TV shows.

I stayed in the trees but kept walking, wishing for a pair of binoculars. It was sunny and bright in the clearing around the house. I stopped and tried to see some movement.

Soon, an old pickup drove down the road from the east. When it got to the building, two men ran out and three others jumped from the truck. All were carrying rifles. I couldn't hear what they were saying, but they quickly headed to the back of the truck.

As four of them stood in a semicircle, the fifth man started dragging a large object out of the truck bed. He reached down and seemed to be unzipping a large bag of some sort. Had they killed this intruder—and was it my pursuer?

What had happened here? Coming from a world where fights tend to be intellectual and usually inconsequential, it was hard for me to comprehend such violence. I crept back into the dense forest and started running away from the fence. I was badly winded in ten minutes and stopped to rest on an overturned log.

Just then, I heard a loud crashing sound in the trees behind me. All I could do was wait for a bullet in my back. I was too tired to do anything else.

18

AS I SAT ANTICIPATING MY DEMISE, I heard a long, low growl and several high-pitched squeaks. That wasn't the sound of an assassin.

I turned my head slowly to the left. A medium sized black bear was standing there sniffing the air. Nearby, barely visible over the brush, were two fat cubs. In a comical imitation of their mother, they were also sniffing the air—or trying to. I had read that bears have bad eyesight—or at least I thought I had read that. As a writer of no special expertise in any one field, I carry a lot of disconnected information around in my head, not all of it accurate.

I kept my eyes fixed on the bears, more transfixed than frightened. It was one of those sights that makes you glad to live in Oregon. Suddenly, the mother bear lowered her head, grunted once, and loped back into the forest, the two cubs following close behind.

What next! Man-eating ants? It had been the kind of day where I was entitled to start talking to myself.

I had a sense of where west was by the occasional glimpses of the ocean on the horizon. In about a half-hour, I came to a logging road. I decided to take a chance that my pursuer wouldn't be materializing anytime soon and walked down the middle of the road—it would be much faster. I turned left to go downhill, figuring that was the way out.

In another ten minutes or so, I heard the loud rattle of a logging truck's diesel engine behind me. The driver stopped the truck, his air brakes hissing loudly.

"Need a ride?"

He was older than the logger I had encountered earlier in the day. It seemed like days ago. He had a round, kind face, slightly red, either from too much sun or too much booze. The faint outline of a scar ran from his mouth to his chin.

"Great. Thanks."

I climbed up into the cab with some effort. All my crashing around had made me stiff.

"Clyde Jester." He reached a big, callused hand across the seat, and we shook so heartily my teeth rattled. He must be in his late fifties, too old to be working this hard.

"Tom Martind . . . Tom Martin."

"Where you headed?"

"To Siletz, I guess. I crashed my car on a washed out road a couple of hours ago over on the other side." I kept the details to a minimum and only gestured vaguely toward the east.

"Geez. You okay? You look a mite messed up."

"Yeah. I'm all right. I guess I kind of got dirty walking around in the forest, trying to get to where I thought I could get help."

"I'm on my regular run to the big mill in Toledo. I've got to get these logs there by two—or I'd take you on into Newport. I could drop you in Siletz. Maybe at the Topaz."

"The Topaz?"

"Yeah. It's a cafe run by the Indians. Good food, good-looking waitresses. You know." He outlined a female form with one hand.

Why Clyde, you old devil. I had noticed he was wearing a wedding ring. He took his foot off the brake pedal, and we rolled forward.

"That would be great. I just need a phone. And I wouldn't mind grabbing a bite, too."

I sat back and relaxed for the first time all day. The scenery was beautiful, and it was nice to be viewing it from a higher than usual vantage point. I also enjoyed being driven for a change. Clyde started humming and I closed my eyes.

"You run into the Cooters up there?"

"Cooters?"

"Yeah, a bunch of brothers. They've got a little farm up in one of them valleys. They call it a farm but, shoot, I can't see how they could raise much. It's too rainy. Parts of the Coast Range are an honest-to-goodness rain forest. Real pretty and green, but all that moisture makes it hard to get anything to grow."

"What do they raise, then?" As if I didn't know.

"Some say it's that mari-wanna. You know, that people smoke to get a nice feeling. Me, I'd rather spend the night with a bottle of Jim Beam and a warm-hearted lady." He smiled and I saw that two teeth were missing, on top in front. He caught me staring and quickly put a hand to his mouth as if to camouflage the gaping hole. "Widder maker done that to my teeth and made me this teeny scar."

"Widow maker?"

"Yeah. That's what we call them in the woods. Every once in a while you run into a tree or a big limb that comes crashing down on you unexpected like, and it's so powerful it kills you. And then your wife is a widder real sudden like."

"God. Dangerous way to make a living."

"That's why I drive now. No more cuttin' trees. I got this from a tree that tied up on me several years back and my chain saw got caught, and when the tree finally went the chainsaw whipped around and caught me in the mouth. You see I was pinned—I mean, my foot got caught under some roots and I couldn't get out of the way. Before you know it, my chin was all smashed up. My Emma, she really got scared and made me promise to start drivin' trucks. A log can still roll over and crush you, but it isn't as likely as long as you tie your load down good."

My neck was hurting from all of this talk about falling trees and demon chain saws.

"What do you do for a living, Tom? Your hand don't feel like it's used to much hard labor." He wasn't mocking me, only curious. But I didn't need to tell him everything. I'd never see him again, so a short version of my life and times would probably do.

"I'm a writer. Doin' some writin' about the coast. I was tryin' to get back to Newport, where I'm stayin'." Kind of fun—dropping those "g's" like Clyde did.

"Int-restin'. Me, I didn't get past the tenth grade. My daddy'd always been in the woods. The money was good and, then, well Emma got pregnant. Here we are. The Topaz in Siletz."

Clyde put on the brakes, and we rolled to a stop in front of a small, neat yellow building. It had sparkling clean windows and a sign that read "Topaz Cafe. Good Eats." I shook hands with Clyde and wished him well. He smiled that goofy, gap-toothed smile of his and waited while I climbed down.

"Good luck, Tom. I'll see you when I see you."

He rolled off after blowing his air horn once. I waved and walked into a truly spotless room. The door had one of those little bells on the top that rings when it opens or closes. I'd always found them rather irritating but somehow, in this setting, it fit perfectly.

The room was lined with booths, the kind with red leatherette seats and plastic-topped tables. I sat down at the one in the corner and faced the room. Only one other patron was in the café—a fat man in a tacky-looking suit sitting at the long counter, stuffing his face with what might have been lemon meringue pie.

A brown-skinned man with black hair tied in a ponytail smiled at me through the pass-through window to the kitchen.

"I'll have more of this, Dianna." The fat man motioned toward the glass case at the end of the counter that held some great-looking pies.

A pretty woman with brown hair walked through the swinging doors from the kitchen carrying a stack of clean plates. She noticed me and smiled. She was wearing a little cap and a uniform with a big hankie in the pocket.

I reached for the menu. It was one of those old-fashioned models where the paper is encased in clear plastic with black fabric edges and brass fittings on the corners. In an era of pretentious menus that are exercises in food hyperbole, this one seemed basic and sparse. "Breakfast served all day" I read on the cover. That was the best news I had had in a while.

"Coffee?" Dianna was at my table. Up close she looked to be about my age.

"Please. Thanks."

She set a heavy pottery mug in front of me and poured the coffee, holding a hand around it to protect my clothing from stray splashes. She apparently hadn't noticed that my clothes were beyond that kind of concern. They were muddy and torn—I was really a mess.

"I'll have the number one breakfast. I guess that's with eggs, hash browns, and hot cakes."

She nodded. "How do you want your eggs?"

"Over hard."

"If you want to . . . a . . . freshen up, the men's room is back through that door."

"Yeah. Thanks. I was in a wreck. Actually, my car got totaled by a washed-out road."

"I saw you get out of Clyde's truck. He pick you up?"

"Yeah. Really saved my life . . ."

A look of alarm crossed her face.

"Not literally. I mean, he saved me from a long walk. He suggested I stop here to eat, and I'll call for a rental car when I'm finished."

"Clyde's a good man. He's my brother-in-law."

"No rental car agencies in Siletz." The fat man was speaking with his mouth full of pie.

We both looked at him, but Dianna spoke first. "We do have phones, Buster, now don't we?"

Buster turned back to finish his coffee, smiling at his little nugget of information. Dianna departed and I went to the men's room to get washed up. The cut over my eye had long since stopped bleeding—it didn't look as bad as I thought it would. I had shaved this morning, so when I combed my hair I looked better than I felt. My clothes were hopeless, however.

Dianna arrived at the table with my food just as I got back. She had placed some napkins and a knife and fork there in my absence.

The food was wonderful—fresh, hot, and cooked perfectly. I ate it all—fast. Luckily, I have always had the metabolism and the height to not have to worry about gaining weight, even when I eat a heavy meal like this—all those eggs and butter and fried batter and syrup.

I was finishing the last bite of pancake when the little bell on the door rang for the first time since I had arrived. In walked two sheriff's deputies, brown Gestapo uniforms and all. They glanced at me and walked over to the counter, then took off their hats and sat on either side of Buster, now on his third or fourth piece of pie. He appeared to have switched to banana cream. He immediately started talking to them in low tones, gesturing from time to time toward me.

I've never been in any trouble with the police, but being around them makes my stomach churn. It always seems like they're going to find me doing something wrong, like driving too fast or having a burned out taillight or something. One of the reasons I liked Angela Pride from the moment I met her was that she didn't make me feel on the verge of arrest.

I wanted to call a rental car agency in Newport, but the pay phone was next to the counter on the far end. I would have to pass the three of them on the way, and they would be able to hear everything I said. I'd just as soon Buster and the two deputies not listen in, even though what I'd be saying would be fairly mundane.

One deputy stood up and walked toward me. It was Troy, the one who had tried to stop me from getting to Susan several days ago outside the center, when she was being arrested.

"You lost, mister? Buster tells me your car got wrecked? Hey, don't I know you? I'm good on faces, but not names."

"We've never met. I know I'd remember." I was trying to ignore him, but he was having none of it.

"I know. I was there when we arrested your girlfriend at the Marine Center last week—arrested her for murder!"

He accentuated the last two words so much that Dianna, Buster, the other deputy, and even the Indian cook looked at me. I got red in the face and took another sip of coffee.

"She isn't my girlfriend. And she didn't kill anyone."

"That's for a judge and jury to decide." He walked away from my table and out the door. I could see through those sparkling, clear windows that he was sitting in his car talking into the radio.

"Shit," I muttered. What was this leading to? Was he calling to see if I was a wanted man? I was too tired for this. I just wanted to get out of here.

"More coffee?" Dianna was back at the table, her coffeepot and splash guard hand at the ready. "Too full for a piece of Diego's pie?"

"Yes. I'd love to have some, but I'm really filled—to the gills."

She leaned over close to me, so the others couldn't hear. "I'm off in twenty minutes. Would you like a ride into Newport?"

I was startled by her offer, but pleased to accept it. "That would be great. You could take me to the car rental place."

She smiled and carried my dirty dishes through the swinging doors to the kitchen. At about that time, the door opened and an older waitress entered, followed by the deputy. She was probably Dianna's replacement. I drank the rest of my coffee and just sat quietly.

In another five minutes or so, Dianna came back through the door wearing a sweater over her uniform. She had taken her cap off. Probably couldn't wait to do that. I handed her the money for the bill, plus a tip.

"Ready to go? Rosa got here early, so we can leave now."

I got to my feet and headed for the door. The deputies made me uneasy in spite of my best efforts to ignore them. She rang up the amount on the cash register and joined me.

"Where ya goin'?" The deputy was up and over to us in a flash.

"I'm giving this nice man a ride to Newport. Any law against that, Troy?"

I remained mute, seeing how this would play out.

"You can't go. I called the sher . . . I mean, if you need a ride, we could drive you after a bit. When we finish our pie, I mean."

"No offense, officer, but I'm looking forward to this nice lady's company."

Obviously, he had called Sheriff Kutler to tell him he'd seen me up here in this unlikely place. The sheriff was probably hauling his fat rear end up here as fast as he could, just to give me a proper Siletz "welcome." He'd be full of questions I really didn't want to answer. But the deputy couldn't detain me, and he knew it. He could only watch helplessly as Dianna and I walked out the door and got into her Datsun pickup.

As we drove past the cafe, I saw the hapless Troy standing on the small porch. Dianna turned and waved, but I just looked straight ahead, trying to erase the smile on my face.

19

FRIDAY, APRIL 24

SOMETHING WOKE ME BEFORE DAWN the next morning. I had set my alarm for seven because I needed to get up early to arrange payment for a rental car until I settled with my insurance company over the loss of my poor old Escort. I rolled over and strained to see the luminous face of my clock.

Four A.M.

I groaned and listened intently to hear the sound. Someone trying to break in? Rain on the roof? No, a low rumble and occasional shouts wafted through the window. I got up and dressed quickly in jeans and a hooded sweatshirt. I ran out the back door and then realized that the commotion was taking place farther down the cove, behind the Phelps house. I crossed the neighboring lots to the top of the cliff overlooking the south end of the cove. Below me, three or four workers bustled around the whale carcass, their work illuminated by klieg lights. The bulldozer idled menacingly to one side.

"Put charges along the body on both sides!"

The voice, magnified by a bullhorn, sounded familiar. I squinted in the dim light to see who was in charge.

Sheriff Art Kutler must have come back from his trip early. He was standing on a rock ledge above the others, like a general directing troops on a field of battle. He only needed a shiny black helmet and a riding crop to look like General Patton. But why was he in charge of a highway department crew? I looked more closely and the situation became clear. The men working around the whale were Kutler's deputies. The highway department was nowhere to be seen. Where was Jake McDowell of the stranding network? For some unknown reason, Kutler had decided to blow up the whale carcass. What was compelling him to repeat the mistake he made years ago just a few miles south? That time, blowing up a whale had turned into a fiasco people still laughed about.

"When those charges are set, pull out and I'll push the plunger," Kutler continued.

Should I try to stop him? Hell, he'd probably arrest me for trespassing on my own property. I'd just have to let the chips— or the blubber—fall where they may. What I wouldn't have given for a television crew.

"Five, four, three, two, one . . ."

I ducked behind a boulder as the sheriff pressed down on the plunger, then covered my ears and waited for the blast, wondering all the while if the flying flesh could reach me here.

The seconds ticked by. No blast.

"God damn it! Who forgot to attach the lines?"

I buried my face in my arm to hide my laughter.

"We're going to have to do this all over again!"

The delay might give me enough time to carry out an idea that had been forming while I lay on the ground.

~ ~ ~

An hour later, just as it was beginning to get light, I returned with reinforcements: Randy Webb, my photographer colleague from the journalism department who worked as a stringer for a Portland television station, and Angela Pride, in all her spit-and-polish state police glory—he to record the scene for posterity (and a TV audience); she to serve as a witness and to keep Kutler from killing me afterward.

Even though I had gotten both of them out of bed, they got there fast. The three of us crept carefully down the path, trying not to make noise and distract the others, who had, by now, gathered around Kutler at the whale's head. So far, they hadn't seen us. After a few minutes, we were ready.

"Art, what the hell are you doing?" said Angela.

Randy switched on his lights and started the camera.

Spotting the three of us, Kutler began to run. But suddenly, he tripped over one of the wires and fell flat on his face. At that moment, one of the other deputies backed away and fell on the plunger. We braced for a deluge of rotten whale flesh, but the blast made only a pop at the head, sending the smelly debris down on the fuming sheriff, who had apparently managed to re-arm only the detonator at that one point. The rest of us—Angela, Randy, the deputies, and me—were shielded from the mess by the whale's body.

That was not the case for Kutler, however. As Randy moved in with his whirring camera, the sheriff got up on all fours, spitting out whale flesh, with pieces of baleen lodged in his hair and blood running down his uniform. After several seconds, he managed to stand and stagger toward the camera.

"I was carrying out the lawful order of Commissioner Davenport to remove the whale carcass," he croaked. "It was creating a public health emergency."

Not to mention harming the commissioner's real estate business and the tourist season, I thought to myself.

Just then, Kutler coughed up more whale flesh and blood and looked about as miserable as I've ever seen anyone look.

He hunched his shoulders as a deputy draped a blanket over him and led him away.

"If I didn't dislike him so much, I'd feel sorry for him," I said to Angela, as we walked up the path. "Anyway, I need to ask you to do something for me. May I stop by your office later?"

"Sure, I'll be in most of the day."

For his part, Randy Webb was beside himself with glee for having the kind of film a television news director would pay good money for. "I can't wait to get on the phone to Portland," he yelled over his shoulder as he raced to his car. "Thanks for thinking of me, Tom."

~   ~   ~

Later that morning, I made several telephone calls to tie up some loose ends on what I had taken to calling the "case." Before I went to see Angela Pride, I had to set up some things.

"Have Mr. Nagamo and Mr. Istook checked out?"

The desk clerk at the Newport Hilton said no, and she'd ring their rooms.

"Mr. Nagamo first."

Before I knew it, Mr. Jima was on the line.

"This is Tom Martindale. I need to talk to your boss."

"He is not available."

"He told me he would help me. I have some information to share with him."

"One moment, please." He put the telephone receiver down, and I could hear muffled talking—in Japanese—in the background.

"Professor Martindale. How may I assist you?" It was the minister himself.

"Thank you for talking to me, Minister Nagamo. I have picked up some information about the death of Professor

Phelps and would like to talk to you about it, in person. It is too sensitive to discuss over the telephone."

"Where can we meet?"

"The hotel dining room is much too public. Do you know where Howard Phelps lives—lived? It's just north of you there at the hotel, off Ocean View Drive near Thirty-third Street."

"Yes. I am sure we will find it. Have no fear of that."

"Good. I will meet you at the house—we can talk inside. How is eight o'clock tonight?"

"That would be satisfactory to me."

I hung up feeling satisfied, although I wasn't sure why. I wanted to get Nagamo to admit his involvement with Phelps—that is, having him on the payroll and getting him to falsify data. I wanted to make public a fact I knew all along: someone other than Susan Foster had a motive to kill Howard Phelps.

What was next? The hotel again. I hadn't stayed on the line as I promised the operator I would.

"Damon Istook's room, please. Thank you."

He answered after one ring.

"Tom Martindale here. We talked the other day."

"Hello, professor. What can I do for you?"

"I need to talk to you about Howard Phelps."

"He's dead. Sorry. Just a little joke. What did you have in mind?"

"I've got some information you may find interesting. About his death."

"What could you know that would interest me?"

"It might have an impact on the whale census figures that Susan Foster was working on."

"Now that would interest me. When do you want to meet? And where?"

"Howard Phelps lived off Ocean View Drive near Thirty-third Street, just north of you at the hotel. I'll see you there at nine o'clock tonight."

"I'll be there."

~   ~   ~

"Is Angela Pride around?"

I was at the front desk of the Oregon State Police office on Highway 101 in Newport. A bored secretary looked up from a desk full of paperwork. Her synthetic clothes did nothing to improve her shapeless body.

"And you are?"

"Tom Martindale."

"About what was this in regards to?"

I would need to remember that sentence for a future grammar lesson for my students.

"She'll know."

"Wait here." She got up with great effort and walked to the back. She had not liked the interruption. I sat down and glanced around at the wanted posters and official-looking memos on the walls.

"Hi, Tom. Come on back. Coffee?"

"Yes, please. Black."

"Mae Ella here will be glad to get us a couple of cups."

Mae Ella's glare was pretty deadly. I sensed a lot of tension between the two women, especially on the secretary's part. I followed the tall, shapely sergeant down a long narrow hall to her sparsely furnished office at the rear.

"Please sit down. Did you come for that information you asked me to get or just to gloat over Art Kutler?"

At that point, Mae Ella stormed into the room, managing to spill some of the coffee in both cups as she set them down hard on the desk between Angela and me.

"Thank you. I hope you got yourself a cup, too," said Angela.

Mae Ella exited abruptly. Although Angela's voice had a cheery tone, her wink at me cast doubt on her sincerity. Patiently, she got several pieces of paper towel out of a drawer and cleaned up the mess.

"Mae Ella has issues with me as a boss." She took a sip of coffee and looked at me for a long time. "May I say something about your tie?"

"Sure, everyone else does."

"The choice of one with the scales of justice on it. Is that a message to me or a comment on the system or what?" She was laughing.

"Unusual ties—some people call them weird ties—are a hobby of mine. I collect them and wear them as a personal statement."

"I thought it had something to do with that. I've got one to add to your collection." She reached into a drawer of her desk and pulled out the perfect tie: it had the chalk outline of a crime scene body that was so familiar to viewers of detective movies and TV shows. "I got it at a police convention."

"Thanks, it's perfect. I'd love to have it. I'll wear it, and think of you and corpses in general."

She laughed again. I liked her—a lot. When would it be all right to ask her out for dinner? Soon, I hoped.

"I spend a lot of my time trying not to end up that way . . . Enough of this nonsense. I guess we'd better get back to business. Were you able to find out anything? I guess you've gathered that I have more than a passing interest in the Phelps case. I mean, beyond any article I'm writing. I'm trying to clear Sue Foster."

"It didn't take a genius to figure that out."

"I don't pretend to be any kind of detective, but I've found that the skills of an investigative reporter sometimes serve the same ends."

"Yeah, I guess you're right. Anyway, here is what I dug up. You understand that this didn't come from me. And, also, that it is harmless enough not to compromise any ongoing investigation."

She pushed a large brown envelope toward me.

"Mind if I look now?"

She shook her head and took another sip of coffee. The envelope contained what looked like summaries of what were probably longer official reports. They dealt with Nagamo, the Eskimos, and Earth and Sea, the environmental group.

"Nothing very incriminating or sinister about any of them. I couldn't find anything on Scott Szabo or your pals Mara and Trog. There is probably more to be known about Nagamo and Jima, but the State Department gets very nervous when we try to get anything on a diplomat or government minister from another country."

"Well, it'll be good background. I appreciate it. Thanks."

"Now, what do you think about this case? I'd like to know."

"Sue's involvement with this case just never added up for me. I decided several days ago that there were a lot of better suspects than Sue. So I've been looking into them."

I told her about my trip to Portland and the visit with Dr. Kirk. I mentioned seeing Scott Szabo, getting knocked on the head in the Powell's parking garage, and being followed to and from Portland and to Corvallis. I mentioned the incident in the journalism department and the unconscious security guard.

She shook her head, as I told my story. "You ever think of changing careers? I mean you could easily become an adventure consultant."

"You probably won't believe me when I say that I don't seek out any of this stuff. It just keeps happening to me."

She raised an eyebrow, then changed the subject. "Do you have any reason to think that this kid Szabo had anything to do with Howard Phelps's death?"

"He was one of his lovers. He apparently sabotaged Szabo's fellowship in New Zealand to keep him in Oregon. I guess Szabo couldn't have been too pleased about that. I also saw someone that looked like him driving down the road just before I found Phelps's body."

"Maybe I'd better take another look at him."

I went on to tell Angela about what I had found out from Anna Garcia and showed her the scrimshaw.

"I can see if the property room in the courthouse has the other half lying around," she said.

"It seems logical that Phelps had it on him when he was killed. If it isn't in his things, maybe the killer took it."

"But why?"

"Maybe as some kind of crude souvenir of the killing?"

"Of course it could be among his effects somewhere—his office or house."

"It's not in the office. I checked."

What was I admitting? Angela was a policewoman, and I was all but confessing to breaking and entering.

"You broke into Phelps's office? Tom, what am I going to do with you? Do you want to wind up in a cell next to Ms. Foster?"

I could feel my face get red, from my neck to the top of my head. My ears were hot too, as they always were when I got caught in a lie as a kid.

"Yeah. I admit it. It was a couple of days ago. I was trying to find out something that would clear Sue. Let me tell you what I did find."

"Going to confess all the way, are we?"

I felt pretty stupid at this point, but I was also angry that I had stumbled into having to tell Angela what I'd found. She was a friend, sort of. But she was also a cop and sworn to uphold the law and all of that. Was "B and E," as they called it, a felony or a misdemeanor? Worse, the sergeant was working with Sheriff Kutler. After what had happened this morning, Kutler would just as soon see me rot in jail as look at me. Oregon's equivalent of Devil's Island would not be good enough for me if he found out what I had done.

"Under the circumstances, will you have to tell your friend Kutler? He'll really be gunning for me after this morning."

"As I told you, I have the primary jurisdiction here because of the nature of the crime. Kutler doesn't like it very much, but I'm calling the shots here. I tell him what he needs to know. After what he did today, I think he'll be keeping a low profile for a while."

"While we're on the subject of my good friend the sheriff, I should probably tell you that I think he came looking for me in Siletz yesterday."

"Siletz. What were you doing there?"

I gave her an abbreviated version of my accident, my pursuer, and what I thought happened to him.

"You really do attract trouble, Tom." She leaned back in her chair and put her hands behind her head, staring at the ceiling.

I finished my story up to the point where I drove off with the waitress, leaving Deputy Troy standing by the door.

"Last time I checked, it wasn't a crime to be in Siletz without a car. If he brings it up, I'll tell him that. I'll look into the latest on the Cooter brothers. We know about them, but we've never been able to make a case stick in court. Murder, of course, is another thing. Now, what else haven't you told me?"

I had no choice but to throw myself onto Angela's good nature. I had to trust her—and I did.

"A while ago, we were talking about my going into Phelps's office. I found two things of interest. One was a folder on his relationship with Andy Kirk. It's in the file drawer in the desk marked 'personal'. The other was material that led me to think that Howard Phelps might be in the pay of the Japanese government. He was getting funding under the table from some kind of research outfit: The Hirakawa Research Fund. I think they paid him to look after their interests, like see to it that whale population numbers were reported high. If there are more whales, they will be classified as less threatened and the Japanese can try to get permission to hunt them."

"Was that ethical, under the circumstances? From what I've read in the papers, the U.S. opposes the Japanese government on whaling. How does that square with what Phelps was doing?"

"It doesn't at all. It means that he was playing one side against the other. He was drawing his salary from the university and getting Federal funding at the same time that he was taking money from a government ostensibly opposed to everything his research was designed to bring about: saving whales. It also means that he was a double-dealing son of a bitch."

"It looks that way," she said.

"Don't you see, though?" I replied. "It expands the list of possible suspects. It moves Sue Foster way down, in my view."

"Not necessarily. She could still get nailed in several ways. She was angry at Phelps for taking the money from a hated enemy—or she wanted in on it herself."

"When I told her about his link with Hirakawa," I added, "she seemed genuinely surprised. I don't think she was faking it. I think I could tell. That was new information for her."

Pride nodded, but said nothing as I continued.

"I'm also wondering about the Eskimos. They have a lot riding on high whale population figures, too. The more whales there are available, the more whales they get to hunt. I can't prove it, but I think Istook is behind the incident in the parking garage. I caught a glimpse of the guy. Although it wasn't Itsook, it was someone wearing a big hat like his guys wear. Also, maybe they were following me in the blue van and white station wagon. Whoever followed me onto that logging road didn't exactly have my best interests in mind."

"You got any proof?"

"Just a hunch. I talked to him, though, and he was friendly enough. He gave me a lot of useful material for my article."

"I guess all of these birds have a motive, but it'll be difficult to prove anything. It seems they've covered their tracks pretty well."

At this point, it seemed safe to omit any reference to the environmentalists. They were probably harmless, if a bit strange. I didn't mention Sue's one night stand with Szabo either. That would only make things more murky. I didn't think it was relevant—at least I hoped it wasn't.

Angela Pride finished her coffee and looked out the window.

"Another thing that clinched it for me," I said, "was when I was in the office, dodging the janitor and anyone else who might find me there, two of the members of the Japanese delegation were outside the window, ready to break in."

I told her about my narrow escape from Mr. Jima.

"We had a report of an attempted break-in, but they didn't make it all the way in," she said. "The guy on night patrol wrote a report, which I saw. After that, I guess it got buried."

"If all of that doesn't cause you to look at other suspects, I'm not sure what will. Sue Foster didn't kill Howard Phelps."

"So you've said." Angela chuckled and shook her head. "You're sure being a terrier on this. Won't let it go. You always this way about things, Tom? Don't answer. I'm sure you are. She's lucky to have you as a friend. If it was up to me, I think I'd release her. She's been indicted, though. That set the wheels of justice in motion, and it'll take more than a state police sergeant to stop them."

"Yeah, I know. But I have a plan, and I hope you'll help me."

"If it involves stretching the rules or putting yourself in danger, Tom, forget it."

"You'll be there, too. I need your help."

"That's why you came here today. You wouldn't have involved me otherwise."

I didn't answer, but the slight smile on my face betrayed my feelings as I outlined what I wanted to do.

~ ~ ~

When I got home later, the sounds of a bulldozer once again drew me to the cliff above the cove. More workers busied themselves with the task of getting rid of the whale. Jake McDowell of the stranding network was standing to one side watching them work. He looked up and waved at me.

Kutler's antics had apparently convinced the highway department to get this job done fast. The men had moved the bulldozer into position to maneuver the whale carcass toward a large hole dug in the sand. The big machine nudged and nudged and, before long, the massive Gray whale began to move. Then, ever so slowly, her remains rolled into the hole and were soon covered by several tons of sand.

20

ANGELA PRIDE HAD GONE ALONG with my plan, I suppose, in part, because she didn't have one of her own. After finding that the other half of the scrimshaw piece was not in the property room, she had agreed to give me the key to Phelps's house. To avoid creating a scene, we decided I would work alone. Police personnel were observing from a hiding place in the grove of trees between my house and Phelps's. Angela was waiting in a cable TV repair truck parked down the road.

I entered the house while it was still light—about seven thirty. As usual for this time of year on the Oregon coast, it was raining.

"I'm in, and I'm turning on the light." I was talking loud enough so the body mike I was wearing would feed my words to the cable TV truck. "I assume you can hear me, but if this is government issue stuff I'll probably short out," I said, always the cynic.

It felt funny to talk like this into the air and not get anything back but silence. As I had noticed a few days ago through the window, the house was very tidy. Phelps had been very particular about his things and, apparently, compulsively neat.

The overturned cup and spilled coffee I had seen through the window several days before had not been cleaned up. For me, this was the tip-off that Phelps had been murdered here at his own kitchen table, not in the lab. He had been too neat not to have cleaned up after himself. But nobody else had given much credence to that theory, however, since they were so convinced that Sue had killed him elsewhere.

The living room led into a hall with a series of closed doors. I opened the first one to find a guest room furnished with a bed, dresser, and chair. The walls were covered with prints of sailing ships. Several glass cabinets contained Phelps's extensive collection of scrimshaw. There were pieces of all sizes, from large sections of ivory to small slices of that material. There were salt shakers and belt buckles—even a cribbage board—all with black etched scenes of whales and tall-masted schooners like *The Pequod* in *Moby Dick*. I didn't see a piece that had been cut in half.

I found my intended destination behind the next door: his study. Except for a large window overlooking the cove and the sea beyond, the walls were completely lined with bookshelves from floor to ceiling. An antique roll-top desk stood slightly out in the room to allow access to books on the shelves behind. I made a mental note to check them out later. They were probably things he didn't use very often.

The desk drawers contained no surprises. I was careful not to mess things up, even though Phelps would never know. Checkbooks, bank statements, stationery supplies. Nothing too exciting. Angela had told me to look in unlikely places for things of interest.

But, under the lower left drawer I found a small antique-looking key taped to the bottom. As I tore it loose, my eyes fell on the lock it no doubt fitted into. A small door in the center of the desk top was situated squarely between the open cubbyholes. The key fit perfectly and the door opened easily, but the compartment was empty! Impossible! Why keep a door locked if there's nothing behind it? I began to feel around the surface of the little space, looking for a latch or spring. At first I had no success. Then, I pushed a carved wooden molding to the left of the hole. Immediately, another small door popped open at the back.

Inside I found two stacks of papers, both held together by rubber bands. I sat down in the desk chair and removed the banding on the first stack. Polaroid photos. In the fading light, I had to squint at the images. I turned on a desk lamp and noticed a large magnifying glass in one of the cubbies.

The scenes were of Andy Kirk and Howard Phelps together and separately in various stages of undress. In half of the shots, Andy was completely nude. Phelps, possibly self-conscious about his aging body, always had something on.

"That dirty bastard. How could a professor betray the trust of a student?"

I was muttering so Angela was probably having a tough time hearing me out in the cable TV van. I didn't necessarily want her to. Would the photos prove that someone other than Sue had a motive to kill Phelps? I wasn't sure, but I packed up the photos and put them in my pocket to give to the sergeant. So much for police thoroughness. I suppose the guys in here were looking for blood or evidence of a struggle and didn't pay attention to anything else.

Now to the other stack. It seemed to be more records dealing with Phelps's involvement with the Japanese. There were accounts of cash transfers from some bank in the Netherlands Antilles. Then there were his own records. By my rough estimate, for five years Phelps had deposited about $250,000 in five banks: two in Oregon, another in New York, and two in California. He had CDs and savings accounts. He lived well, but not any better than other full professors. He must have planned to spend it later, after an early retirement.

"You're going to love this," I said out loud.

"Talking to yourself, professor?"

I didn't need to turn my head to know that the Japanese delegation had arrived.

"It's a habit of people who live alone. Good evening, Mr. Nagamo. You're early. It's only seven forty-five."

"I learned punctuality as a child. It's a trait that is highly regarded in my country; less so in yours. I will have those papers, please."

"I didn't ask you to meet me here to discuss these papers!"

"On the contrary, you have found what I have been looking for. You've saved me a great deal of trouble, professor."

Nagamo snapped his fingers once and Mr. Jima appeared in the doorway.

"Please hand them to my colleague."

At that, he pulled a small revolver from his pocket. I'd never had anyone pull a gun on me before. I reacted like I do when I see a scary movie: a chill went down my spine and my eyes started to burn.

"All right. You win," I said in as calm a voice as I could muster for Angela Pride's benefit. She was probably trying to calculate the danger as she listened on her earphones. I hadn't gotten enough out of Nagamo yet. I wanted to draw him out more and hoped Angela would hold off barging in.

Jima crossed the room and took the records. Thankfully, Nagamo didn't ask him to search me. I wanted to pat my pocket for reassurance that the photos were there, but didn't dare.

"Can't we all sit down and talk this over? And would you mind pointing the gun in another direction? It's making me a bit nervous. I promise not to do anything stupid. Take the papers with my good wishes."

Nagamo relaxed and sat down in a chair near the door, his bodyguard standing beside him, arms folded across his massive chest. The smaller man reached up and took the packet of records. He didn't look at them, but stuffed them in the inside pocket of his suit coat.

"Aren't you going to examine them? Or do you already know what they contain?" I asked him.

"I have a general idea. They are the last tangible evidence of my government's link with Professor Phelps. A most disagreeable person, that Phelps."

"Is that why you had him killed?"

Might as well come out with it. No sense beating around the bush. I wanted to get his answer on tape—even if I wasn't around to hear the playback.

Nagamo was surprisingly calm when he answered. "My government is not in the business of killing people who, as you Americans say, double-cross us. I know there are other ways to handle such a greedy and demanding person. Even after the professor was unable to alter the numbers on the Foster study, he still wanted full payment. He had failed in his mission, but didn't seem to realize it."

"But the numbers were higher in the second report. That meant he did what you wanted him to do."

"We created that report," said Nagamo, "and left it here for him to use at the conference the next day. We expected him to substitute the new figures for the ones presented by Miss Foster. If not for our actions, he would have failed in his mission completely."

"How long had your government been paying him?"

"Our arrangement goes back five years, since we started having trouble getting permission from the International Whaling Commission to kill whales. But the arrangement ended with Professor Phelps's death. Now, no one will be—as you Americans say—the wiser. I have all the records."

As he patted his pocket, I decided to stall for time, hoping Angela Pride would move in.

"Why kill whales at all? Only a fraction of your people still eat whale meat or even like it."

"We have killed whales for centuries. They have been part of our very existence. Why should a great nation like Japan have to get permission from weak-kneed conservationists to do something we have every right to do?"

"Because what you are doing is wrong!"

"We had this argument before, professor. About whales and cows and chickens. It is very tiresome to repeat it again. It is a futile argument. We will never be on the same side of this issue, I fear. Americans are too entranced by these creatures, these whales."

"I can't argue with you about that. What are you going to do with me?"

"You will remain calm and . . ."

At that moment, the house went dark. Jima let out a grunt of surprise. I could hear him stumble out of the room and down the hall. Then I heard a gasp and a thud, then nothing. Nagamo and I sat waiting. I wondered what he had done with the gun.

It was too dark to see anything. I had nothing to ignite—no lighter, no matches, not even my trusty penlight. Suddenly, a brief flash of light broke the darkness, then I heard Nagamo moan and, apparently, fall over onto the floor.

Now it was my turn to be attacked.

In an instant, the intruder had grabbed me by the arms, whirled me around and ripped all the recorder paraphernalia off my body. The tape really stung as, one by one, the various connections were disengaged. He had my arm behind me and was dragging me out of the room and into the hall. He did not utter a word.

Neither did I. As he bent my arm higher up my back, I could feel the blade of a knife at my throat.

21

I WAS STILL NOT ABLE TO SEE WELL ENOUGH to identify the attacker dragging me across the yard.

How long would it take Angela to figure out what had happened? I wanted her to arrive with a SWAT team at any moment. Nothing.

Who was this guy? Scott Szabo? Damon Istook? Whoever he was, he was in great shape. Despite the need to be walking for us both, he wasn't even breathing heavily. As we started down the crumbling path to the floor of the cove, I caught sight of a black ski mask. In fact, he was dressed completely in black. He pushed me hard as we started down the path, tightening the pressure on my arm just enough so I wouldn't fall. I half hoped I would lose my balance so we both would careen to the ground.

Where was Angela? The roar of the sea would muffle the sound of my voice, so I didn't even try to cry out.

Within minutes, we were standing on the floor of the cove. The tide must have been coming in because half the beach area was now covered with water. I looked toward the small arch to the north in the direction of my rented house. So near and yet so far. Why had I let myself get into this mess?

The larger arch opening was to the sea. This was how the beached whale had gotten into her predicament. The rough sea water had propelled her through the arch and onto the beach at high tide. It was easy to see how treacherous the ocean could be in here. The water wasn't all that deep, but the power of the waves was magnified as they were forced through the opening. Anything being pushed through would be battered against the jagged rocks of the cove and injured fairly fast. That was exactly what was going to happen to us if I didn't think of something to do. The sea was rapidly getting closer. And it was really rough.

My kidnapper suddenly let go and pushed me to my knees. I crawled over to a bunch of low rocks at the rear of the cove and turned around to face him. He was tall and well-built and strong. My arm was probably bruised from the pressure he had been putting on it. I rubbed it to regain circulation.

"I want you to know that this is not personal, Martindale," he shouted over the roar of the waves.

The shouting exaggerated the sound of his voice. I could not identify it.

"At least you should let me know who you are. You owe me that much."

"What do we have here, a reporter's curiosity? Didn't you know that curiosity killed the cat!" He paused for a moment and then ripped off his mask.

"Dr. Kirk! Why go after me? I had nothing to do with Andy's death."

The roar of the ocean quieted, and I could suddenly hear him more clearly.

"Howard Phelps killed my son. He pushed him overboard . . . or paid someone else to push him." Kirk wiped a hand across his face. His eyes were wild. "Andy was too sensitive for this world. He was so ashamed of what Phelps did to him, maybe he jumped overboard." Kirk was talking in circles and not making any sense.

"You don't know what happened on the ship, but you killed Phelps? Why let Sue take the fall?"

"I don't blame you for trying to stall for time, Tom. But you can forget any idea that the police will be here to help you. They have been called to the scene of a very bad traffic accident on Highway 101."

Kirk had thought of everything.

"Since we're tying up loose ends here, doctor, how did you know I'd be wearing a wire tonight?"

"Just a lucky guess. Plus, I noticed you seemed awfully friendly with that attractive state police officer. Earlier you asked me a question about Ms. Foster. It was nothing personal, believe me. She was a convenient scapegoat, nothing more. I needed somebody to divert suspicion from me, in case the police went down that road. When your friends, the Japanese, substituted new figures, that gave her even more of a motive—I mean, it cast doubt on her as a scientist."

"It boggles my mind that you have been able to keep track of all of this—to pull all the strings so masterfully."

"Let's just say I've made it a point to know where you were and what you were doing by keeping my eyes and ears open."

"So, you killed him in his house. But why did he let you in?"

"When he saw me on the deck, he opened the door. Once I got inside, there wasn't much he could do to stop me. He wasn't all that strong."

"Did you want to have it out with him or were you looking for something?"

"Records of his dealings with the Japanese, for one thing." Kirk hesitated. He seemed to be deciding whether to tell me something else. "I guess I can tell you. You won't be around to tell anyone."

That caught me by surprise. Up until then, he seemed so rational I thought I might survive this. But I decided I had nothing to lose in continuing. "What else did Phelps have that you wanted?"

"Polaroid photos of him and Andy. When I heard about them, I knew I had to get them and take care of that old pervert for good." Just talking about Phelps and the photos made Kirk angry all over again. I needed to calm him down.

"After you killed him, you dragged him down here?"

"Yeah, and I almost got caught. Some blond kid with a beard came up on the deck and tried the door just after I'd hit old Howard over the head."

"Scott Szabo," I muttered. I'd been wrong about him, too. A gust of wind sent foam from the churning water swirling up into the air like tiny snowballs.

"What did you say? I can't hear a blasted thing in all this wind."

"I said it was another of Phelps's students, Scott Szabo."

"Another student he ruined?"

I didn't answer because whatever I said would just make him angrier. That would put Szabo at Phelps's house earlier than I had seen him. That didn't make sense. The wind died down at that point so I could hear Kirk better.

"Damn kid came back again, when I finished with the body down here in the cove. He kept yelling Phelps's name. In fact, he was still yelling when I slipped out that arch and got out of here."

He gestured toward the north wall of the cove. That answered my question. Scott Szabo was in the clear. I changed the subject.

"Why did you put the body in the whale's mouth? Were you trying for something symbolic with that, doctor? Were you making some kind of statement to the world?"

"That was part of it, I guess. But the whale was really just a convenient place to hide the body. I hoped the carcass would float out to sea and the body would never be discovered."

"What do you want with all these records?"

"I guess I considered it further evidence of Phelps's dishonor in everything he did. The man was evil. I wanted the world to see that as clearly as I did."

"Did you follow me to Eugene—and back?"

"When you brought me up to date on things at my house in Portland, I decided you might be getting too close to the truth. You are very persistent, Tom. I needed to keep a close watch on you. I just couldn't be sure what you might do next."

"It was you on the logging road? I didn't recognize the car. Don't you have a Mercedes?"

"Yes. I picked up that old junker station wagon to throw you off. I hadn't counted on having to follow you on those back roads or that your car would go into the ravine. For a day or so, I thought my Tom problem had been solved."

He wasn't kidding. As we talked, it became clearer and clearer to me that the solution to his "Tom problem" would result in only one thing: my death.

"So you were trying to find me to kill me?" I tried to keep my voice calm.

"Not at first. I just wanted to figure out what you knew."

"I have you tell you, Dr. Kirk, that you worried for nothing. I didn't have a clue as to who you were."

"I couldn't take the chance."

I changed the subject. "What about the Cooter brothers—I mean the pot growers who captured you? I thought they'd killed you."

"You saw all that? They surprised me with that trip wire. Once it went off, they came at me from all directions. They tied me up and carted me off to their house. When they found out I was a doctor, they asked me to treat some guy with an infected foot. After I'd done that, they let me go. They took me back to my car, and I drove out the way I came in."

"But didn't they worry you'd turn them in?"

"I got the impression that they were used to dealing with the police. It didn't seem to bother them. I think they figured I had things to hide, too."

Kirk stopped talking. He seemed to be relaxing a bit and dropped his arms to his sides. I guess he could see that in my exhausted state, I was no threat to him. He seemed to be uncertain as to what he would do next.

As he talked, I could see a large form behind him trying to come through the arch from the open sea. Although members of a whale pod often return to aid stranded comrades, it had been over a week since the Gray had gone aground. Now it was buried. This seemed highly unlikely.

But it wasn't.

The medium size whale let out a shriek so loud that Kirk jerked around. Then he lost his balance and fell. At that moment, a large wave came roaring into the cove. For reasons endlessly studied by oceanographers, every seventh wave is bigger than the six waves coming before. These are called sneaker waves because they catch people unawares. Signs warning of sneaker waves dot the Oregon coast from Gold Beach to Astoria.

Such a wave hit Kirk. I was able to scramble up the rocks, but it was too late for him. The wave overtook him and pulled him rapidly under the water and out toward the arch. In a matter of moments, he was gone. In all the commotion, I lost sight of the whale. It had apparently moved away from the shore again. What instinct had compelled it to come back to the spot where its compatriot had lost her life? Was it concern or curiosity or some kind of strange revenge?

After the huge wave retreated, the waters became strangely calm. I got down from the rocks and walked to the water's edge. The waves were gently lapping at the shore. As I looked down into the water, something caught my eye. The light from the just rising moon was glinting on something in the finely ground sand at my feet.

I reached down and picked it up. It was the other half of Andy Kirk's scrimshaw piece. I felt for its mate and then dropped my discovery inside as well. Above me, the mournful cries of circling gulls were a reminder of everyone who had ever been lost at sea.

EPILOGUE

SATURDAY, MAY 9

AFTER I TOLD MY STORY TO THE DISTRICT ATTORNEY, Susan Foster was released.

She immediately went to Boston to spend a week with her mother and recover from her ordeal. Except for a brief telephone conversation when she called to thank me, we hadn't spoken about anything that happened, until today.

She and I were meeting Angela Pride for coffee at The Whale's Tale, a funky restaurant on Newport's Bay Front. I had chosen the place, very appropriate given the role that mammal had played in all that had happened to the three of us the month before.

Angela was sitting at a table near the back as I walked in. I was glad to see she was dressed in civilian clothes—a polo shirt and khaki skirt that did wonders for her figure.

"Morning, Angela. Tell me, have you ever had even so much as one speck of dirt on you?"

"It isn't allowed in the Oregon State Police manual." She smiled, pleased at her unusual stab at humor. "I've ordered some cinnamon rolls."

"Sounds good. Sue should be here soon. I didn't actually speak to her, but our machines traded messages."

A waitress poured my coffee, and I reached for a roll. Angela and I looked up at the sound of the door, as Susan came in and looked around for us. I stood up and waved.

"Sorry to be late. I had trouble parking."

I got up and pulled out her chair. As she sat down I noticed that she seemed, at first glance anyway, to have recovered from her time in jail.

"This may sound funny," I said, "but have the two of you ever met?"

"Actually no," said Angela, who reached out her hand. "I only saw you in court from a distance."

"I didn't really notice anything or anyone then," Susan replied grimly. "I'm glad to get the chance to meet you, too—finally. I want to thank you for doing so much to help me."

The waitress poured her coffee.

"It wasn't that I did so much, I just didn't stop Tom from all of his harebrained schemes to prove your innocence."

I looked at them both in mock innocence and held out my hands, palms up.

"I'm paid to be skeptical of everyone," Angela continued, "but the facts in your case just didn't add up, as Detective Sherlock here kept telling me."

We all laughed. I looked over at Sue as she sipped her coffee.

"May I ask a question?" she said. "Where was Howard actually killed?"

"We think Dr. Kirk followed him home after the two of them argued in Phelps's office," Angela said, then turned to me. "That meeting you overheard, Tom."

I nodded.

"Phelps must have gone home to get a copy of the fake report," she continued. "They argued and then Kirk hit Phelps over the head with the hammer, one he had taken from your lab. After the doctor disposed of the body, he went back to your lab and planted the report and the hammer. I guess he didn't notice that the cover had been torn off, perhaps as Phelps struggled with Kirk or fell down."

"How did he get in?" Sue asked.

"We're not entirely sure," said Angela. "Maybe by talking the janitor into opening the door for him."

"I think we know the rest of it, as far as the good doctor is concerned," I said. "Has his body washed ashore anywhere?"

"I've alerted police agencies all up and down the coast, but nothing yet."

"What about the Japanese men?"

"Minister Nagamo was only wounded in the attack. He pleaded diplomatic immunity in answer to my questions. After he recovered, he was quickly and quietly returned to Japan after the State Department intervened. His bodyguard Mr. Jima was killed by Kirk in the attack."

"And the Eskimo, Damon Istook?"

"He returned to Alaska. He arrived late for his meeting with you and left when he saw the house dark. He admitted that some of his overzealous compatriots had attacked you in the parking garage and followed you to Corvallis. They even knocked out the security guard. They were trying to shake you up. Istook said he would deal with them in tribal court."

"I don't know about that young environmentalist—Mara," I said. "She didn't finish the course and no one has seen her around the center. I asked the director's secretary."

"I've had news of another student, Tom," added Susan. "When I got back to town, there was a message from Anna Garcia. She wants me to help her renew her scholarship."

"Great, I hope she comes back to school."

"Speaking of students," Angela said, turning to me. "That kid you suspected of being the killer, Scott what's-his-name?"

"Szabo," Sue and I said in unison.

"When I called to tell him he was no longer under suspicion, the housing director said he had moved out and dropped out of school."

"That's right," said Susan. "I saw . . . er . . . I talked to him when I was on my trip." She wasn't looking at me as she spoke. "He's gone back to California."

Were they seeing one another again? It sounded that way, but I didn't really care.

"I have to ask you about Sheriff Kutler, Angela," I said. "How's he going to survive all that bad publicity? The pictures of him flailing around in all that whale blubber were all over the news for a week."

"I think his days as a public servant are about over. He's taken some sick leave for now to reassess. The other commissioners are pretty ticked at Davenport for pressuring Art and at Art for agreeing to do what he did. I'll be surprised if he runs for reelection."

"What a shame," I said in a mocking, insincere tone. "What a loss to law enforcement. Well, I guess that does it here." I was making the first move to end the meeting. I got up and shook Angela's hand. Sue still did not look at me, so I decided to force things a bit.

"I hope we can see one another under better circumstances, Angela. I mean, like dinner? Okay if I call you?"

"I'd love it," she answered, glancing at Susan as she spoke.

"Great, I'll do it soon. Thanks for all you've done for me."

"And for me, too," Susan added, looking forlornly from Angela to me.

I left money for the check on the table, and the three of us walked out to the sidewalk. The street was bustling with the usual weekend mix of tourists, cannery workers, and fishermen.

Impulsively, I hugged Angela and kissed her on the mouth. She reciprocated without hesitation. I hugged Susan, but no kiss. My little revenge.

"You bastard, Tom," she whispered in my ear.

She dropped her arms and we parted. The three of us went our separate ways. I walked east toward the docks where the fishing fleet ties up. As I made my way along, I caught that wonderful sea smell that always conjured up the images I love. Instinctively, I reached into my pocket and pulled out the two halves of scrimshaw. I often rub them for good luck and as a reminder of the power of the sea and all the creatures in it.